The Takeback
A Vampire's Revenge

J.H. Dean

Harry G Publishing—Triangle, VA
ISBN: 979-8-9874875-0-1
Library of Congress Control Number: 2023900906
Title: *The Takeback: A Vampire's Revenge*
Author: J.H. Dean
Digital distribution | 2023
Paperback | 2023

Dedication

This book is dedicated to all of those who love and miss classic gothic writing. Those who are encapsulated by the art given to us by authors such as Bram Stoker, Mary Shelley and Anne Rice. I wanted to try and bring back the darkness and lure of the classic vampire novel. I hope to influence another generation of readers and do justice to the genre.

I also want to dedicate the book to my wife, family and friends that encouraged and supported me through the entire process of bringing this novel to life. Without their support, and contribution it may never have become a reality. I would like to encourage anyone who has a dream of writing and publishing to do so and never stop dreaming until it's a reality in their lives.

Last, but not least I want to dedicate this to all of you who purchased this novel and supported my dream. There are millions of books to choose from and you picking mine is very special and will never be taken for granted. Your support will encourage me to continue the path of writing and publishing. I may never be a Stephen King or Daniel Steele but my success is based on your enjoyment of this book. Thank you all very much and I wish you and your families much success and happiness.

Chapter 1
Awakening

The night air above must be frigid since the ground that surrounds me is extremely cold. I do not know if it is night or day, but it does not matter. I do, so long to reach the surface and soon I will. My paralysis has almost worn off and I will soon start my escape from this prison I have been in for so long.

The challenge is using what energy and strength I have left to dig my way out and start looking to regain my full strength. I have been here many years unable to feed or call out to anyone for help. My body has endured years of neglect. I can only imagine how bad I look based on how I feel. The lack of feeding has left me weak and frail. My skin has shrunk around my frame. My eyes feel as though they will pop out of their sockets.

My lips are stretched thin and all I taste is dirt. I long to taste something fresh and warm. My nails and hair have grown uncontrollably like weeds left unattended. I am so thin you can probably see right through me in the right light. This has been a torture I would never wish on any person except the one who did this to me.

He deserves the same hell I endured just existing year after year unable to move, unable to live. Your life going by without you in it. He should have to feel the emptiness and helplessness that comes with being stuck in this situation. He should be the one waiting to just die, frustrated that death never comes. The only thing that comes is the thirst, the uncontrollable thirst to feed and sustain yourself. The desire to live because the instinct to survive is stronger than the situation you are stuck in, but you are not able to answer the call. You are just plagued with the misery knowing you could be stuck like this for eternity.

I have many things on my mind that will need to be done once I am mobile again, but revenge is very much my focus. He will pay for the years I spent lying here and I will regain what is mine. He made a mistake of not just killing me. He may have thought it was easier to get rid of me short term so he can get what he wants. That was a mistake he will regret and unlike him I will finish the job and leave no loose ends. He and everyone who helped him will pay for this betrayal. There will be no graves, and no prisons to confine them.

Chapter 2
The Escape

The more I think about my revenge the more strength I find to help with my escape from this shallow prison I have been in for so long. It will be for not if I am not able to recover and if I am not able to find him and reclaim what I worked so hard for. I do not know what awaits me or how much the world has changed in my absence.

I will have to travel by shadows until I completely regenerate. The sight of me now would scare people and I do not need that kind of attention. I will deal with that in time but now I must start my escape. The process takes time, but most important thing is to escape and get the blood running through my veins again.

I begin scratching and clawing my way to the surface. It is hard because I am extremely weak and unable to really put effort into this escape. When I finally break the surface the night air is colder than I thought but it is embracing me like an old friend. I am thankful that it is not daytime, I would have burned into dust halfway out of the ground. Then all my efforts would have been for nothing.

The fresh air hitting my lungs is amazing, and it is moist with night dew. I can feel some of my senses refiring and my body starting to reawaken. There is a slight fog around me which will give me some help hiding in the shadows. I can see what looks like the exit and I recognize where I am. There was not as many graves here when I was imprisoned and to see a grave with no tombstone with no name is rather sobering. It is like being erased from history. It is amazing that all these graves were added around me, but I was never accidentally dug up. It seems like whoever runs this cemetery knows where I was and purposely avoided me. I will need to research this area and confront whoever it is that helped keep me locked up here.

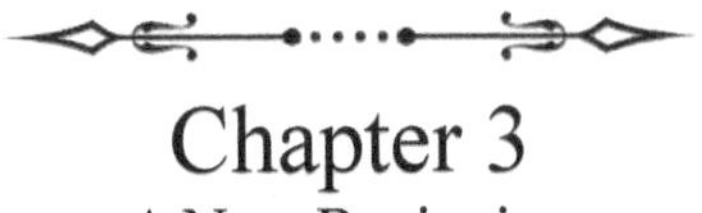

Chapter 3
A New Beginning

I make my way to the road, after several minutes. The area looks a lot different than when I last saw it. I am not sure how much time has passed but the area has changed. The road is no longer made of dirt and a lot of the woods seem to have been removed, and little houses are spread across the land. I will go in the direction of the town I remember from the past.

I have a house and I hope it is still here. I need to find a place to hide by morning if it is gone. I really need to feed. I am so weak that it is making it hard to reach town. I must keep moving though I can't afford to get stuck out in the open. My senses are weak, but I pick up the smell of a mortal. It has to be close since I am so weak, and my sense of smell is far from good. It is taking me in the right direction though.

I slowly make my way toward the scent, but I also am getting faint smells of wine. This smell makes me think of days of drinking cheap wine with her and how much I still miss that. I can easily get lost in thoughts of her, but I must stay focused on the task at hand. The scent is getting stronger, and I can almost taste the meal waiting.

I finally find the source of the scent I am following. It is an elderly man asleep on the side of the road. The smell of wine is coming from him, and I can tell he is sleeping very heavily. He looks like life was not kind to him and that wine seems to be his out. I have seen this a few times, but most men did this behind closed doors. It is very disgraceful, and I figured no one would miss him.

He is very dirty, and his clothes are old and torn. He has a long dirty beard and long dirty hair. His footwear is ripped and held together by ropes. He is dressed warm enough but looks as if he has his clothes packed with other things to stay warm out here. He does not seem to have anything but a half bottle of wine.

His face is red and dried out. You can tell the weather and time have not been kind to him. He looks older than he probably is, but I almost felt bad that no one loved him enough to help. These thoughts really are not important, but my mortality will not let go and I always find myself too connected to what I am doing instead of just doing.

I can approach him without any trouble since he is passed out. The only problem is I need to get him into the woods. I do not feel strong enough but if I was to feed, I will find the strength. I reach down and quickly pick him up and move toward the woods. He seems extremely heavy, but I need the blood, and nothing can stop me.

I gently lay him on the ground behind a big tree and bit into his neck. The rush of blood hitting my lips and surging through my veins was like an intense rush. The rush of blood is almost like getting drunk from wine and can last longer than getting drunk. The wine mixed in his blood really leaves me a little off, but it is worth how good it felt to feed after all this time.

It did not take long for my veins to recover and my skin to start loosening. I can feel my body start to awaken and my senses start to be sharpened. I want to keep drinking but I know I cannot feed after his heart stops. I know I must release him, but it feels so good to indulge on fresh human blood. It will take time and more feeding to really get back to a healthy condition. I really hate feeding on humans, but it is the only source of nutrition for me especially in this condition.

Chapter 4
Home Sweet Home

I left the old man in the woods and continue down the road toward town. I figure I can find one more meal before morning, so I focus on that thought. I get a little way down the road when I am startled by an unfamiliar sound. I can hear voices then I see lights coming toward me in the dark night. I make my way back away from the road into the shadows where I can watch from a safe distance.

Then to my surprise a carriage makes its way past me but there are no horses. The carriage is moving itself down the road and the people travel as if it is natural. It is a beautiful machine that seems to move effortlessly. It is black and white with gold lights mounted on the front. Beautiful wood frames with what seems to be rubber mounted to them. There is also beautiful hardware mounted to several places on the frame.

I do however find the noise very off putting but the ease for which you can travel makes it worth learning about. It could speed up my travels from place to place while I am here in town. I realize I am spending too much time watching this machine and forget I need to get to town because daylight is quickly approaching. Town is close now, so I need to just hurry my way there and stop getting distracted.

I make my way around to my old place. The building

is closed and boarded up. The houses around my house are also boarded up. The town has grown, and this part was forgotten over time. The grass is waist high, and the trees and bushes are overgrown. The houses are covered in dirt and damaged from time. I am just hoping my casket is still in place and that the house is better inside than it is outside.

I go around to the backside of the house. The paint is cracked and faded. The roof appears to be in bad shape and ready to fall in. The window I need to go in has several inches of grass and weeds in front of it. I can easily reach through that and pull the wood off the broken window. It looks as if it was purposely smashed in by someone.

Once inside I make my way down the hall and the weather damage inside the house is disappointing. The inside is unlivable and there is a horrible stench in the air. The doors are faded, and the paint blistered. The furniture is all covered in sheets and a lot is missing. I am happy to find my casket still in good condition, and where I left it so many years ago. It appears to be in good shape, but I will know more when I open it and get in to sleep the day away.

Moment of truth I slowly open the casket and it holds together. Slowly I climb in the casket and lay down. I hear a lot of noise but figure it is from not being opened in many years. Then I pull the lid down and settle into place to rest. Then to my despair the casket collapses around me. I do not have time to get a new one or find another shelter, so I have to make do with the pieces I have. Clearly my first task is acquiring a new casket and getting it in place.

Chapter 5
A Better Night's Sleep

Arising early in the evening I realize it is still day but with the overcast and the sun setting it should be safe enough to venture out. I have two tasks to focus on this evening. The first was a suitable meal to continue my recovery and the second of course is getting a casket to rest in tomorrow. I may need to get two depending on where my journey takes me.

I start out into the night my thoughts wander to revenge and finding him, but my recovery will take time and I need to be at full strength if I am to fight. I feel at home in the brisk night air. It welcomes me back as if I never left. It is a true gift to be able to walk the night after everything I have been through. The night brings a surprise this evening that I was not expecting. I am in search of a meal, and I do not think the town would be so overpopulated. This I figure will make it hard to feed but as I walk, I pick up the same scent as I left the cemetery.

I track the scent down to its source out in the woods just outside of town. There is a small caravan of old guys camping in the woods. They all seem intoxicated just like the older gentlemen I fed on last night. I know I can take them, but it might be better to wait until they pass out. This will allow me to take one or two a night if they stay here.

I'll wait but I really want to take them all so they will not get away. They will know something is wrong if they start disappearing one by one, so I'll just wait and take one after they pass out. I am gambling but they will not remember anything and hopefully they think he just wandered off. Only time will tell of course.

This feeding should give me what I need to get back to full strength. I head into town to find a casket. There are more people than I was expecting to run into. This town has grown since I was here before. I cannot stay out too long because the day will be coming soon and waiting out the drunk guys wasted a lot of time.

I now only need to focus on the task at hand, but my mind always goes back to I need to get revenge. He must pay for what he has done. The Vampire is forbidden to kill each other; it is how we survive. I have no way of knowing if someone knows what he has done and if he has been punished. If he did get away with it, he could have turned on someone else and got himself killed. Honestly, I hope none of it happened and I get a chance to finish him myself.

I know greed pushes him and revenge will push me to do what needs to be done. It does pain me that I must kill someone I considered a true friend. The part of my humanity that is left makes me second guess my vampire nature but eventually I know I will have to give in and accept who I am. I need a lot of information to find him and to finish this chapter of my life.

My wandering has paid off and I find a shop where caskets are made. I can see into the building and there is an old pine casket sitting in the back outside area of the store. I will help myself to the casket and I leave a small note stating I will return to pay for the casket the next day. It is a long walk back to the house and I will look crazy carrying a casket if anyone sees me, but I do not have a choice. I move as quickly as possible and stay within the shadows as much as I can until I reach my house.

I spend several minutes putting the casket in place and the sun is starting to rise outside, it is time to try my new bed. My mind of course is only focused on what has happened and what is to come. I really think I might regret digging up the past and think I might find things I will regret. Betrayal can run deep, and you never know what you will find out. A million scenarios run through my mind, and it is hard to rest but it is necessary to regain my strength. I just hope he knows his time is short.

Chapter 6
The Journey Begins

When I was imprisoned I had businesses and assets not joined to our businesses. I figure I will have some money to carry me depending on what happened after I disappeared. He may have taken everything and moved. My first few days I will spend looking for clues of him, and of myself. The only way to fund my journey is to find my assets that he may have in his possession. I find nothing in the area; it is like we never existed. I have no way of tracking anything because too much time has passed.

I realize I must start from scratch and will need to rebuild wealth. I will need to first attend to my appearance and the few jewels I found in the house will not sustain me for very long. I will have to find a way to make money and rebuild my empire. I need to find a place at night to work and I will need a way to travel. These are the vital things to help with my journey.

Tonight, before returning to the caravan of men in the woods, I get a haircut and purchase new clothing. I am also hoping to find employment while I am out here searching. I will also continue my search for anything to link me to my past. After a while I find no job or anything useful in town. I then return to the camp and have a meal before returning to my poor excuse for a home.

After a good day's rest I am ready to go out and make some progress. I need a job and a new place to live so that I do not have to worry about my place collapsing on me. Finding a job at night is hard and finding people to work with and trust is even harder for people like me. I have built an empire from scratch before, and I have to do it again.

With the town being so built up now it gives me a unique advantage that I never had before and should make things easier to obtain what I need. I still have to hide my identity except to who I truly need to help me. This is going to be a real journey but if I succeed it will be well worth the headaches.

Chapter 7
A Lucky Find

I think maybe I can get work at the docks at night, this will allow me to earn money and find a ship I can travel on without being detected. I can talk straight to the ship's captain and make a business deal with him. The docks to my bad luck are empty and there are not many ships here, but I figure this gives me lots of time to study all the ships going in and out of here. Wind coming off the water like it is now always catches my attention and how I miss it. How I miss the coolness of the breeze blowing off it. Then out of the blue I see what appears to be the shadow of a person on another one of the ships and decided I must go check it out.

I quickly make my way over to the ship's deck and search the whole ship. I find nothing even after calling out to whomever it is. I will stay a few more minutes then, I will leave a note for one of the boat captains to meet with me the next evening. I start for home, and I take the long way so I can get a better feel for the area I now live in.

My trip home is anything but normal because as I make my way down the road, I pick up a strange presence. The presence of another vampire quickly came upon me and has followed me most the way down the road. I stop and call out but there again is no response. I search the whole area and turn up nothing.

I am not sure what he or she wants or if they are even following me, so I just dismiss it and keep walking.

The night came quickly, and I head back to the docks with hope the captain will be waiting for me. I hope not to startle him, but I need to secure transportation then another casket to put onboard the ship. This will allow me to travel safely and without any problems from the crew. I will of course need to head back to the casket shop to obtain another casket.

I met up with the ship's captain and after a very lengthy conversation he agrees to allow me to ride along on his ship unbothered if I do not do anything to his crew members and if I help him, when possible, with work on and off the boat. This is of course is a perfect situation for me to get my financial situation straightened out and it will allow me to travel and investigate my past.

With travel secured I head back to the casket shop to acquire another casket for the boat. I am pretty sure it is going to be an awkward conversation, but it is a necessary one. I hope to get a good deal but since I took the last one without permission it might not go so well. The shop is about to close when I arrive, and the shopkeeper does not at first want to talk to me. Then I explain I have gems for the casket from out back that I had taken.

I then explain I need another casket and that I will pay him, or I can do work around the shop to help pay for the casket. I try explaining I can only work nights while I am in town. At first, he does not want to help then I explain to him that if he does not help, I will have no choice but to kill him and take what I need.

At this point I make it known that I am a vampire

and that I will have no problem taking what I want but I would rather have a business partner I can trust and work with. I gave him several minutes to think about it as I look over the inventory he has on hand. As I expect we come to a mutual agreement that will help me further my rebuilding process. I tell him I can run the shop at night and even help build products to sell. We then load a casket onto a wagon he has and take it down to the dock. I am then able to take the casket onboard and set it up as the shop keeper rides off back towards the shop.

After loading the casket, I head back to the ship's deck where I am planning on just relaxing a bit to take in the fresh air coming off the water. As I stand there overlooking the water the presence from earlier returns and seems closer than before. I scan the area but find no one and no one responds when I call out to them. This is getting frustrating since I should be able to easily find them.

The presence follows me most the way back towards my house, but day is approaching and tomorrow I will be going to see an old friend. I need to figure out who is following me, but it will wait until I return in a few days. Hopefully I will have more time and information when I return. I was not sure before, but I can say for sure now this person is following me, and they just may regret it soon.

Chapter 8
An Old Friend

The presence that had been following me catches me tonight as I enter the campsite to look for another meal. I should try to find them, but I really do not have time to deal with this. Eventually we will come face to face no more games. The trip is about two days and hopefully there will be a stowaway that I can use if I get thirsty. Stowaways are great for that purpose because most of them are not expected at a certain time or dock and can easily disappear with no questions asked. I will only feed, if necessary, otherwise I will be in my casket or up on deck just enjoying the ocean air. The journey should be interesting because the captain is the only one who knows me and why I am onboard.

I sleep most of the first day and when I awake there is a bad storm brewing, and the waves are hitting the boat hard. Lightning and rain surround us on all sides. The wind is blowing like a hurricane and make moans like an old man lying in bed days before he dies. The captain handles the ship well and even though it is a bad storm he pulls us through like it is nothing. His few crew members I come across do look at me funny, but no one questions me. I just keep to myself and listen to the storm from my casket room most of the night.

The second night is beautiful and quiet, so I spend a good portion of the night on deck. I speak to the captain for a while then make formal introductions to the rest of the crew. Then the captain gives me a list of things I can do to help the crew for the rest of the journey. I am pleased to help since he is not charging me to ride with him and his crew. I think this will also put the crew at ease to see me working alongside them. I explain to the captain I will be getting off at the next dock and will reboard the next time he docks here.

As I leave the area near the docks, I see it has built up quite a bit. I barely recognize any of the city with all the new businesses and homes. The main road is the same, so I just follow it out of town towards the countryside. It is a couple hours to my friend's home if he is still there so I will just try to stay on track and not get lost in thought. The countryside always reminds me of her, and it makes it hard to just ignore what I still feel.

The walk is nice and quiet but then about forty minutes into the walk the presence from home appears out of nowhere. I stop on the road and scan the open areas around me and all the tree lines but once again find nothing. I am truly irritated by this person, but I do not have the time to look for them, so I just keep moving down the road. The presence does not leave me until I reach the main split in the road where I need to turn and head toward the oldest part of the countryside.

I am about ten minutes away from the house and the wind picks up and the night air chills a bit. I can feel a shift in the night and a familiar presence is there before I can react. I am grabbed by the neck. His nails bury in my throat as my blood trickles down his fingers, he quickly steps back then grabs me up in a hug. He is startled to see me and apologizes for the rude welcome back to the area. Then he laughs saying I am slow and that he could have easily killed me, he wants to know why I was slow to react and where I have been. I told him there was no time to talk now that we need to get back to his place quickly.

We reach his house in a matter of minutes then after settling I ask him for help with a couple things. First, I ask him if he has seen or heard of Phillip in my absence and second, I ask if he is up to trying to catch someone who is following me for the last couple days. He said of course he will help me catch whoever is following me, but he wants to know why I did not know where Phillip is and why I need his help with information on him.

Chapter 9
Catching Up

The reason for my absence and the reason I am in need of help with information on Phillip is the same I explain to him. Phillip has double crossed me many years ago and left me for dead in a shallow unmarked grave. I think greed pushed him to do it, but I am not sure exactly what caused him to turn on me. We had built a nice empire and we were living well with several businesses and houses. We had everything we needed and more and we had spent many years together travelling and exploring what we were and why vampires existed.

Then one night I left the office a bit early and was walking home just enjoying a quiet night when out of the blue he attacked me and knocked me out. When I came to, I was lying in a shallow grave, and he looked me in the eyes as he drove a stake into my chest. He then laughed as he covered me up with the dirt that became my prison for many years. There were no signs of unhappiness or anger he just snapped for no reason as far as I can tell.

I need information because in my time of imprisonment he disappeared and so did our businesses. I need to recapture what was taken from me so many years ago. I also told him about the outbreak of new vampires, and they seem to be untrained and have no discipline at all. I feel like we need to get control of them and teach them how to live our lifestyle properly. In not so many words he tells me they are not my responsibility and that I need to just worry about what I was searching for. I understand his point and then explain to him I will travel back when I leave here to deal with them. He then says he will travel with me to deal with the new bloods. That should be enough to clean it up, a couple of elder vampires with no patience for untrained vampires that jeopardize us all.

We set out towards the old cemetery. This will be a good starting point for us to try and start tracking down the one who follows me. We walk slowly at a good distance from one another back toward the docks. We walk for hours and find nothing. The presence usually pops up near the docks but there was nothing this time. We decide to spread out and head back towards his house before day could catch up to us.

As we make our way back, he asks for more details about what has happened to me and what I was planning on doing when and if I find Phillip. I tell him my plan is simple, find him, get back my businesses and then I will rid the world of him. He deserves to pay for what he has done.

The torture I endured because of the blood cravings and the daily haunting of my mortal life was more than anyone can bare, and I could not escape it. I will make sure he feels every bit of the pain and suffering that I did. Wherever he is, his time is short, and he has no idea what is coming for him!

We were not far from his place when he laughs and said you never told me how you were brought over to the night originally. To answer his question meant going back and reliving the emotional and physical pain I endured during and after being brought over to the night. I told him I would explain to him later how I was brought over but first we must sleep. There is a lot to do tomorrow, and I figure we will need all the energy we can muster. Laughing he says it might help me to talk about it and we have lots of time considering who we are.

Chapter 10
The Recap

I start the story talking about how my wife Reina and I would take walks at night around the neighborhood. We would always end up at an empty field near our house where we would sit and discuss our day. The field was by our house but still a good distance, so it was good exercise and enough time to really talk. It was at that field that I saw her for the last time.

I remember like it was yesterday, and it haunts me still to this day. It was a still night, and the moon was shining big and bright up in the sky. There was no wind and there were no clouds in sight. We started out on our usual walk to the field and like two teenagers in love we were talking and joking without a care in the world. The only sounds you could hear were our voices and the nighttime bugs in the area.

We were not too far from the field when we thought we heard something and so we stopped and looked around. We did not see anything, so we continued walking toward the field. We reached the entrance to the field when we heard a voice from the trees laughing and then in a malicious voice it sounded out how wonderful our blood would taste. We quickly turned around and started running back toward the main road without hesitation. It was in vain because before I knew it, I was waking up on the sidewalk and my wife was gone.

I stood up and started searching the area and yelling at the top of my lungs for her. There was nothing, not even a small trace as to where she went. I could not explain her missing and I immediately started blaming myself and it was not until later I would find the answer to her missing. I spent several weeks with several people doing a manhunt for her, and we turned up nothing. Then I decided one evening to head back alone to the field to search one more time for something to help me.

I reached the field about the same time as we did the night she vanished, and I spent several minutes searching for clues. Then out of nowhere the same voice came through the trees saying I should have learned my lesson about coming to this field. Then there was laughter as if to poke fun at me. Then before I could react, I was pushed to the ground again as if he was just playing with me.

Then as I stood up there was silence as if he had left and I was standing alone again. Then suddenly, I was hit in the face with something. It left me a bit stunned. It took me a minute then I looked around and found nothing in the field and no one in the field. Then as I started to walk back out a glitter on the ground caught my eye. I bent down to find my wife's wedding ring. This of course sent a shiver down my spine and made me realize I may never see her again. Right then I was done looking and realized I had nothing else to justify me continuing to search for her.

At that moment I decided to sell everything and move somewhere new to start over. I needed to be far away from here so I could start to move on and put this life behind me. I moved to a small town and took up a new job as a metal worker. I figured this would keep me busy and help me stop thinking about her. The shop was also near a seaport so I figured it would open more business opportunities for me. It was also going to allow me to meet more people and build a network that would help me move on also.

I found the work, as busy as it was, did not keep my mind from wandering back to her. Sometimes I could still smell her and feel her next to me. My depression was not helped at all and so I started drinking every night at the local pub. The more I drank the more nightmares I had and the more I saw her face around town. I had the overwhelming feeling that she was alive but there was nothing I could do about it.

Chapter 11
The Evolution

Then one day as I was clearing my shop a small boy appeared and asked me for help. He told me he needed some metal work and that it was extremely important . I told him I could do the work, but I need to know what materials and designs he was looking at. Then I turned to grab some paper to write down notes and when I turned back, he was gone. He left on the counter some jewels and detailed instructions on what he needed. The paper also had directions to the house where the work was to be done.

With him stating the importance of the work I unpacked my tools and got to work right then. The work was some small metal pieces, but they were very detailed. The designs seemed like artwork more than just some accessories he needed. I really studied the examples, and they seemed rather morbid. They were very dark, but they were very beautiful. That night I did not leave until all the cutting and molding was done. The second night I did all the detailed work and polishing of the pieces. Then I packed them away for the journey out to the property.

The night of the second day after completing the work I had a nightmare of Reina with the guy in the drawing. They were sitting in a lonesome cold graveyard filled with ancient tombstones. The moon was high and big in the sky. The clouds were looking menacing and dark. In the dream Reina was standing behind the man and she seemed scared. The biggest of the metal plates I had made was being worn as a chest plate and the man seemed to be royalty. Then as he stood and moved towards me, I awoke and realized it wasn't real.

The next evening, I did a final check of my work and gathered all my equipment and some extra supplies that I might need during the install. I was hoping that doing a great job would bring me more work moving forward. My biggest concern when I was heading out was, what was I attaching these to and was it made from quality materials.

I was not sure how long it was going to take to reach the property so I headed out as soon as I could. The walk was nice and gave me time to just enjoy it like I used to do. I was walking and not really paying attention as I went down the road. I almost walked past the address because I was not focused. The area was nice but seemed empty like no one lived out here and the driveway was long and made of dirt.

I approached the house, and it was beautiful and old like European design. It seemed out of place out here but with the amount of European influence in the area it is not shocking. The yard was not well maintained and there were vines on the house as if it was deserted, but to my surprise the door opened before I could even knock. The boy was standing there and ushered me into the house and shut the door behind me. He then quickly moved me into another room.

From this room he moved me again into another room down a small flight of stairs. This room was dark and very large. There were no lights, just a lot of candles lit throughout. Besides the candles there was nothing but a large casket sitting on a base in the middle of the room.

As I moved to study the casket the boy handed me another set of instructions on how the pieces were to be placed on the casket. The instructions also included polishing the entire casket once the work was finished. I turned to ask the boy a question and he was gone again just like at the shop.

I started studying the casket and found there were already amazing pieces on the casket and the work seemed to be very old-world style. There was also a very good etching in the dark wood of the casket. The etching was of a man, and it was the same man in the designs I was given by the boy. I had also had dreams of the same man and it was him just laughing. There were also gold pieces of metal including the hinges that were in perfect condition.

The stand seemed old as well, but it was covered in a lacy black cloth. I realized my work was expected to last as long. This casket seemed to be generations old with many different eras of work covering it, as if it was passed down from family member to family member. I found it weird because usually the casket would be in the ground not transported around from location to location. I suppose it did not really matter so I began working on placing the metal work onto the casket. It took me hours to complete but I really enjoyed myself and completely lost track of time. I realized I really loved this work and I hope to make a life of this work.

I finished up and cleaned the casket then grabbed my tools and headed for the door. Then from behind me I heard a weird noise and so I turned to see him face to face. The man from the casket, and from the etchings. He was alive and well it seemed. I was bewildered since I thought I was alone and there was only one door in and out of the coffin room. I was just not sure what to do so I said hello.

At first, he said nothing, just staring at me with the light flickering off his unique and piercing eyes. As I watched him move into the light you could see his eyes were green and his lips were red like wine. His face was white, and his bone structure was model like. He was very well dressed and very tall. He appeared to be athletic to best describe him. Then with a strong French accent he began to thank me for the work I had done on the casket. He smiled and asked if the payment I received was enough to cover the work. I told him that the jewels more than covered the work especially since it was such an honor working on such a beautiful item.

He smiled once again and said he was pleased to hear that but that he had one more thing to add to my payment. I was going to decline any further payment but what he gave me was not money at all. He grabbed me and bit into my neck and drained my blood. I felt myself dying and it scared me. He was so strong, and I could not do anything to defend myself.

He told me to not be scared and just rest when he finished. Then he said I was not going to die, that I was going to live forever. He then put his arm to my mouth and told me to drink the blood coming from an open cut he had made on his arm. I felt as if I had no choice and so I began to drink from his arm. That feeling was nothing short of ecstasy. I had never felt anything like it before and I have never felt anything like it since.

Every cell in my body exploded and I just craved that feeling without thinking about it like an animal. I just wanted to keep drinking but I felt his heart and mine start beating and slowing together. He got upset and threw me off and he disappeared. I just lay there for a few minutes before everything went black.

Chapter 12
The New Beginning

When I awoke it was dark and cold like I had never experienced before, and I was confused. I was not sure where I was or how to get out of wherever it was. I started to panic then I calmed myself and realized I was in some sort of casket. I then concentrated and pushed up on the lid until it opened into more darkness. I climbed out of the casket and felt my way around the room until I located a door. I pushed my way through the darkness and up to the family room. The house was dark and cold just like the basement. Everyone seemed to be gone and I thought that I must have had a bad dream.

I sat down on the couch and just pondered what was going on and what was real. I sat there for a while then a thirst came over me that I had never felt. I did not know what was going on or how to deal with it. I was not sure what was going on, so I started searching the house for answers. I was hoping to find something to help point me in the right direction. I mean what was happening and what I was becoming, I was scared and unsure. I searched the house and the thirst got worse and I was really feeling like this was not a gift but a curse. A curse I did not know how to deal with and that I didn't want.

After an exhausting search I found a note in the casket room. The casket was still in place, but he was clearly gone. The note was a detailed report or set of rules if you wish. It explained to me that I was now a child of the night, a servant of blood. He had given me the gift of immortality and that I was now ready to face the world from a different perspective.

The letter went on to explain the rules and the day-to-day activities I should expect moving forward. The letter was very clear on a few things such as, I would never crave or need human food again. I also would need to sleep in a casket or somewhere completely hidden from the sun due to the fact it can kill us. He went on to explain that I should sleep during the day and then head out at night and feed away from where I live. He said that feeding would take practice but to never drink after the heart slows or stops. It could make me sick and ruin my night. I started thinking maybe this gift was anything but, only time will tell.

The letter was short and to the point, so I headed out into the night alone and confused. I was not sure what changes to expect. It did not take long for me to immediately see the difference in my senses. Everything was clearer and sharper. The night had a different feel to it. It was like I was finally home. I felt like a teenager again and I had never felt so strong before. I also had never had such a thirst before either. That's when I realized the change to my teeth and that my new lifeline began there.

I walked for a long time and then I came across an old man minding his own business. I, without even thinking about it, jumped the guy and drug him out of sight. I latched on to him and this was my first real human blood feeding. It was simply amazing how much I loved this and how much it quenched my thirst.

I was in extreme ecstasy and almost forgot to stop drinking. All I could think, or feel was how our hearts got in sync as I drained his body. When I was done, I was still in need of more and had to find more tonight. I was left wondering how much I need, how many people each night to quench my thirst. Where would I find enough people to keep me going for a while.

Chapter 13
The Search Begins

I realized I did not have enough time to seek out another poor soul to feed on, so I headed home. I did not want the day to creep up on me and make it for a very bad morning. I did not like the idea of sleeping in a casket so I would need to find another way to sleep and protect myself. Then I realized going home would not help me so I needed to go back to the house where I could look for more information.

The next evening, I searched the house for any information that might help me. I was not sure what I was looking for exactly but there did not seem to be anything. I guess the next step would be looking for another vampire that could help me. Then I paused for a second to collect my thoughts and Peter speaks up before I start to say he wants to hear more. He wants to know how I gained so much knowledge and understanding of the vampire world. He also wants to know how I met Phillip and the whole story of that part of my journey to here. I tell him we should take a break and we can talk more, and I will discuss his story also. He agrees while laughing that we can discuss things more and we can get back to focusing on the project at hand. We really need to find out what is going on and protect our way of life. We figure the only way to stop and fix this is to find the coven and stop them. Then I can finally focus on finding Phillip.

Peter and I head out into the night to find the young ones. We are not sure where to look, so we split up and search in different areas of the city. We agree to meet up after an hour of searching. Then as we met up we pick up the scent and presence of another. We follow the scent to the edge of the city.

This is an isolated part of the city because it is the home of many of the people with disabilities or with growth challenges. This is a smart place to hunt since this area is so isolated and the inhabitants cannot defend themselves. We are not here to stop them but to watch from the shadows. Whatever happens we must let it unfold so we can follow them back to the hold up. They did not seem to see or sense us, so it is easy to keep up with them and get a head count. This small group was two males and two females. I recognize some of them as workers from the local plantation. This made even more sense that these are people no one would miss are being turned. I was not sure if we can get through to them or not, but we wait and follow them after they fed.

Chapter 14
The First Confrontation

We follow them to an abandoned business in the middle of town. They are hiding in plain sight. The building is not hidden at all and has no protection from outsiders. That is how it appears from the outside. We wait and continue to watch from the shadows. We really need a head count so we can try and figure out what we are facing inside. The group we followed met up with another small group just outside the building. Then as they are talking the doors open and a large man steps out onto the landing. He instructs them all to come inside and they did just that.

We left for the day and figure we will come back the next night to watch and learn more about the pack we are about to confront. As we make our way back to Peter's he explains that the building use to belong to his family. Then an out of towner had recently purchased the property and they did not think anything of it. They did find it weird no business had been started or did not appear to have been started there. We now know why, and hopefully we can end this peacefully.

We had been waiting about an hour and I was getting impatient and was about to leave but Peter says just relax. Then all of them come out of the building and start down the road together. Then the one we figure to be the leader splits and goes on his own. I follow him while Peter follows the group. We agree we will not confront them until they are back at the business and on their turf. We think they will be more comfortable that way.

I follow the leader back to the edge of town. I guess the group explained the town to the leader or maybe they rotate their feeding grounds. The guy just watches from the shadows for a while. The townspeople are starting to close their businesses and head home. Then I notice he is following a woman that has gone off by herself. The road led deep back in the woods and completely hidden from everything. He follows a lot further back than I expect him to. I figure he will attack right out of the sight of everyone. Then just before he attacks her, he laughs out loud and yells *woogley e woogley*. I am completely confused by this. The woman though is completely afraid and screams out loud in vain. You can see the terror come over her whole body. Her face turns white, and she starts to shake. She turns and tries to run but it is too late.

He quickly grabs her and begins to drain her without remorse. I can feel their heart beats and smell the blood as it leaks down her neck. It takes everything I have not to jump out and try to take her for myself. He finishes drinking then tosses her limp body in the woods like trash. We then head back to town, and he does not take any more victims. I find it odd but at least there is only one life lost tonight. His walk back seems to take forever but I catch up with Peter about the same time the others meet up.

We sit and discuss what has happened while we were separated. Peter tells me they had basically taken out a whole ship and then torched it leaving the bodies to burn inside. Then they just head back here like nothing happened. We decide we need to stop them now, so they do not destroy the only transportation in and out of town. We move towards them out of the shadows. We want to reach them before they go inside. The group is taken by surprise and start to become aggressive. We try talking to them and explaining that we are just like them and that we need to discuss what has been happening here in town.

We try to get them to talk so we can explain to them what changes they need to make to benefit all our kind, not just their coven. Then they surround us, and the leader approaches from behind the group. I know Peter and I are more than strong enough to take them out, but we do not want to. Then the leader of the group says we are foolish to approach them uninvited and for sticking our nose in their business.

I then reply to him that they are the foolish ones and if they do not listen and do as we say that this will end badly for them. I also explain we are looking for information that they may have. Information that could help us stop whoever it is that is creating so many vampires in this area. I then try to offer help and guidance to them since they are a young group of vampires. He then laughs and says that they do not need help from outsiders and that it was now time for us to die. Peter and I try to avoid a fight and we try to warn them one last time.

Then they approach and Peter and I look at each other and start laughing, they do not understand why we are laughing but they are about to find out. The more we laugh the madder they get which of course helps us distract them. The leader snarls and heads towards me saying he is going to destroy me. Then the rest of the group heads towards Peter on the other side, we are outnumbered but not out manned. Before he can touch me, I grab him and throw him up against the building. Dirt and dust go flying from behind him, then I pin him against the wall. I then repeat to him no one must die tonight, if you just back down and listen.

He tells me to piss off and he grabs me and tries to push me off. I do not allow that to happen and then Peter grabs the rest one by one and throws them into the building busting out the front door. Wood, dirt, and blood go flying everywhere. Then I grab the leader and pick him straight off the ground and slam him down to the concrete. I give him one more chance to surrender and listen with the understanding everyone in his pack will die now if he declines.

He again tells me to go to hell and that he will not surrender so I nod to Peter. Peter grabs one of them and snaps their neck like a pencil. His face changes and he then realizes that we mean business and that he has no choice but to cooperate. He speaks up and tells the rest to stand down and he begs me not to kill anyone else. He then agrees to cooperate if we let them go. I tell him we want to help but we need information. He once again agrees if I will let him up.

I agree and back up slowly as he rises to his feet. Then he starts laughing and says woogley e woogley again and before he can turn around, I put my hand through his body and rip his heart out. His body drops to the ground as blood runs down my arm. The rest of his crew run off visibly terrified with no idea of what just happened. I look at Peter and we nod at each other, and we follow and finish off all but one of them. They forced our hand, and we can show no mercy for arrogant people who think they are unstoppable. We then take the one back to the business and tie him up so we can rest for the day. It never feels good to kill people who have no idea what they are doing, but we cannot allow anything to disturb our home.

Chapter 15
The Friendship Begins

The night is good for interrogating the last of the coven to try and get any information I can find. He has nothing to share with us and has no value to justify keeping him. We decide to just kill him and burn down the building. This will leave no evidence about what has happened here. We do not need any more attention to our community or what we are capable of, so it is best to end it here. Killing others is forbidden but in this situation, it is for the betterment of our kind. These vampires should have never existed.

I start to head out, but Peter talks me into staying a few more days so we can look for more information. He also wants to hear more of my story. I tell him we may cover some of it but since we are a couple hundred years old, we could be here forever. He says he would like to know how I met Phillip since that is what I am working on now. I say fine and start by saying I met Phillip after being a vampire only a couple weeks. I knew nothing so I followed him since I had nothing better to do.

I start my story off explaining that like the newbies we just killed, I was changed and left to fend for myself. I did not know what I was going to do but I had to figure something out. I travelled at night and with my wife gone and now this change I figured I should just go back home and start over. I needed safe passage back home, so I was scouring the docks looking for a boat that goes out at night.

I found nothing at the docks and started to head out when I heard a laugh, then a cold breeze flew past me. I scanned the area quickly to see what was going on. This was just like when my wife was taken and without warning I was grabbed, but this time was different I was able to grab back and slam him to the ground. He started laughing again, I snarled and asked him what was so damn funny.

He just continued to laugh as he explained that he figured I must be a new vampire since I did not pick up that he was following me. He explained that the tingling sensation going up and down your spine is an indication that a vampire is nearby. You should also be able to smell the difference between humans and vampires. He also explained he did not want to hurt me, just test me for strength and awareness. He wanted to gage my personality and temperament. I backed up and told him to be careful when he gets up, I will tear him to shreds.

He slowly got up and backed up away from me still smiling. He dusted himself off and asked me what I was doing down here, and why I seemed so lost. I explained to him that I really didn't know I was just trying to get home from here. I also was looking for information on what or who we are and what I am supposed to do. I didn't even know vampires really existed until recently.

He proceeded to tell me he had a boat and that he would love to have a travel buddy if I was up to crossing the oceans. He said he also heard rumors about a guy in Romania that may have a lot of good information. He was supposed to be a real old vampire that had lived for a thousand years. It was only rumors, but he thought it would be a great journey we could embark on and try to find him.

I thought about his offer for a while and then decided I had no other plans. I agreed to travel to Romania with him if it was beneficial to me there was no reason not to.

Chapter 16
The Search for Dracula Begins

The vampire went by the name of Dracula and we must do research about where we will be travelling so we can get in and out without any problems. A library would be a great place to start looking then we will plan our trip and head out. We sailed out the following evening and even though I did not trust him I did not have much of a choice. I needed safe passage and he had that covered for us. The bottom of the ship was sealed so we could anchor during the day and sleep safely.

The trip was long and there was a lot of stuff we studied on the ship. He also showed me how to feed without killing our prey so it would last us a long time. We had maps and locations of Dracula and all the castles he was associated with. The countryside is a tough trek, but we knew we could do it better than a mortal could. The storms of the ocean will be a huge challenge for the old boat, but Phillip said it has been through far worse.

The first day at sea our ship was hijacked by pirates as we slept. They left a small crew of eight to navigate the ship back to port after emptying it clean. They somehow missed us in the hull. That night when we woke, we quickly realized what had happened and we had to take the ship back. We dispatched the first six pirates quickly, but it was still daylight, and we had to wait for the remaining two to come below deck or for the sun to go away. Once they were dispatched, we started to fix course towards Romania but had no maps to navigate with.

We anchored the third night knowing that there were four locations we would be visiting and that it was a long journey through the countryside. We did not know where to start so we figured we would get our bearings and hit them as we got to them. We would have to use the resources of the locals in order to find our way. Our hope of course is that this journey is not in vain and that we find lots of good information to take back with us. It was still night but day was upon us so we stayed on the ship until next evening so we could safely dock the ship.

We docked early the next night and went onshore. We spent time on the docks and found help from a local fisherman. Seems we had landed in France and was still a day's journey from Romania by sea. We were not happy but with no navigation tools we were lucky to have made it where we were. We spent the evening looking for food and supplies. Then we boarded the ship and shoved off heading toward the Mediterranean Sea. This was the main passage to the Black Sea passing the south side of Greece.

We made a good distance through the night but had to anchor for the daytime. I was excited as I lay down because the possibilities of what lies ahead of us were endless. I was filled with anticipation and hoping the outcome does not let me down. Phillip is more worried about what he can steal and return home with. The artifacts we will find may give us a lot of clues to our history, so I am not upset about it. Finding Dracula would be the best outcome for us if he really existed.

Our final dock was in the city of Constanta, Romania. It is one of the few seaports in the area and is supposed to be busy. We should be able to get good information there so we can start off on a good foot with our journey through Romania. The evening came rather quickly and so did the storm of storms. We could not pull anchor due to the high waves and the winds rocking the ship like a rag doll. I wasn't sure if we would make it through the storm but we just stayed put in the hull and discussed what we were going to focus on so we could maximize our time and distance. After several hours the storm disappeared, and we were able to move into the Black Sea. The storm was almost like a warning to stay away but we did not listen and as we approached Constanta another severe storm moved in and blocked our way to shore. It wasn't not safe to drop anchor where we were, so we had to float and wait out the storm. We had the luck of seeing lights on the docks from a good distance which could guide us in.

Chapter 17
Romania Awaits

We docked early in the evening and made our way into the main part of the port city. We found that the most interesting and important castle of Dracula was Bran Castle. This castle lay in the countryside North East of the docks and was a good journey by foot. We also found out that no one had seen or ever been able to locate Dracula in the years since his imprisonment. There are a lot of rumors and hearsay about the man and the myth. We were hoping to find the truth Dracula was supposedly the emperor named Vlad the Impaler a viscous ruler who was responsible for thousands of deaths. He apparently died and was reborn as Dracula.

We found two other castles linked to Dracula and they were Poenari Castle and Hunyard Castle where Vlad was imprisoned. We rested through the next evening before starting up into the countryside. Finding him was the key we needed and hopefully we do not leave disappointed.

With a map we found in town we started out staying as close as we could to buildings and places we could hide if we did not make it by daylight. We walked for a long time before the castle came into sight. It was truly a beautiful structure. I had never seen architecture like this and so detailed. I could feel the anxiety building as the castle was coming closer. We were excited about what or whom we may find inside what was once the jail of such a madman. He was a true tyrant that would kill you as quickly as he would look at you. He wanted power and control and knew no boundaries.

Hunyad castle is the last place associated to his rule since it ended here. This castle has sat vacant for hundreds of years according to the stories so the inside of the castle should be interesting. What could be waiting for us if the stories are true is the most powerful of our kind that is known. He could of course just destroy us for disturbing him uninvited. It is unlikely he would hide here but you never know what survival instincts will make you do.

As we reached the doors, I did not feel the presence of anyone else and I really did not expect to even if he was here. The main doors of the property seem to be of great value, hard wood, hand carved and must weigh hundreds of pounds each. This was just the beginning of the wonder of this castle. The towering rooftops and the design of the open walkways are breathtaking considering the age of the property and the amount of time it was vacant. Hearing about this castle and seeing the pictures, does not stack up to experiencing this in person.

After admiring the outside of the building, we went in the front doors not sure what we would find but ready for just about anything. What we found on the inside was amazing and it felt like walking back in time. The furniture, tapestries, and carpets all seemed to be centuries old. With a light layer of dust covering everything you could tell no one had been here in many years. The place felt abandoned and yet still felt like a home. It was the strangest thing to feel like you are walking into someone's home.

The first floor turned up nothing interesting but a real nice library and a kitchen full of very nice chinaware. The bedrooms were left as if someone was returning, and the bathroom seemed to be ready for them. No running water but the tub and the sinks with the proper towels and shave kits were still set up. The boiling pot and water buckets still sit at the ready and the changing screens sit in the corner just outside the tub area. As we moved down the halls the beds in the rooms were still made and clothes laid out as if they were waiting to be worn the next day. We found nothing useful but everything interesting.

We then decide to descend into the basement floors of the castle. We were not sure how many floors there were, but we needed to find a safe place we could rest for the day. It took forever to find a lantern to light our way since the castle was pitch black especially once you headed down the staircase into the next floor. We found rooms with no light coming in that we could sleep and hopefully be undisturbed until evening. It was nice to lay on a bed instead of an old casket.

The next evening, we scoured the next couple floors until we came to what seemed to be the last floor of the castle. We started down a dark hallway that led into a cave under the castle. The stone and brick stopped, and it was a rock cave on the side of the mountain. The path leads to a couple of rooms with shelves carved into the walls. There were pots lining the shelves and several caskets in the middle of the rooms. This appeared to be a vault of some kind. None of the markings were familiar. We had no idea what they said or what family was entombed here. We were looking for anything that pointed to Vlad or Dracula. We found nothing that was useful in the tomb, so we decided to head back out to the upper levels of the castle. We hoped to find something in the library that would be helpful.

We spent several hours going through the library to find nothing. This main castle turned up nothing to help our journey. We needed to spend one more day here then we will head out to the next castle on the list. We were not sure how far the castle was but we had an idea in what direction to walk so hopefully we do not get lost along the way. We had time but no one to help along the way and of course we had no idea if there would be shelter along the way.

Chapter 18
Poenari Castle and Bran Castle

We headed south east the next evening at dusk. The castle was called Poenari but the locals called it Poenari Citadel. It was a property Vlad the Impaler acquired and built into a fortress to protect his empire during war. We did not know what to expect because the pictures we found showed a collapsed property with not much to look forward to. We were hoping to find some buried secrets in the castle that would give us some clues to Vlad or our kind.

The walk was dark and eerie because the forest and the mountain side had a personality all its own. I am sure during the day it would be a beautiful hike through the countryside, but we will never experience that for ourselves. There did not seem to be a general path to follow so we did the best we could do, until we found what seemed to be a main road through the town. After several minutes on the main road the silhouette of the castle on the horizon. It was a very large place and very intimidating. This would explain why it was used as a fortress and an anchor for Vlad's territory.

The darkness could not hide the fact that time had been brutal to the castle walls. Several of them had crumbled and left the inside courtyards exposed. Any building left abandoned as long as this one, can easily be destroyed by the elements and vandals. Something this important should have been protected and kept up. Historic architecture should always be preserved. I did expect the inside to be as bad as the outside, but time was not on our side this evening and we need to find shelter. There is a lot of ground to cover and who knows if there are hidden places not mapped out inside.

The next night was boring since most of the valuables had been removed and not much remained of the fortress from the time of Vlad's rule. There should have been a lot more evidence of him, but it was like the history of this place was erased and the castle was left with no identity. As beautiful as it is outside, the inside was twice as nice and it's a shame to see it in this state. Unfortunately, just like the other castle we were unable to find anything useful and left us with only one more place to check within the circle of Vlad's influence.

The last castle is Bran Castle due north of where we were. We are not sure how much of him remains in the castle but hopefully we find some evidence. We also are not sure exactly how far the castle was so we would be walking blind until we reached it. Hopefully we find the walking path that leads to the front gate.

The castle was farther than expected. Luckily, we found shelter for the daytime. The next evening, we found our way to the front gate of the castle. We made our way to the main doorway to enter the castle's main building. We were startled by a woman and her son camping in the front room. She was startled and scared but I assured her we were not going to harm them. I also explained we were archeologists and we're here to survey the castle and look for some specific artifacts. Then we headed towards the back wing of the castle.

I headed down the steps and Phillip headed up the other stairs. We figured we would cover more ground if we split up. I made my way to the dungeon area of the castle and into what appeared to be an armory of some kind. The place was basically cleaned out apart from old furniture. I spent several hours and turned up nothing. I returned upstairs and to my dismay I found the lady and her child drained on the floor. Phillip is out of control, and I am not sure if it is my problem.

We spent the last few hours and turned up nothing. We decided to stay here until we could safely travel back toward the docks. There were a couple graveyards we could check out on the way back and maybe that would turn up something helpful for us. This trip so far has been a bust and I regret making the trip here with Phillip because of the senseless killing he has done. I guess each of us deals with our situation in a different way. Eventually I guess he will calm down and use better judgement. I find it funny that we have found nothing related to vampires or the fact that Vlad was in fact a vampire.

Chapter 19
Lost Cemeteries

We made our way to the first cemetery and found nothing but an old graveyard with not very many graves and no vaults or mausoleums. There was no shelter and no evidence of vampires or anything that would help us. We didn't spend a lot of time here because we didn't want to delay getting to the next location hoping to find shelter for the day. As we approached the gate, we could see statues and large headstones. This looked promising because it was a large area with lots of crypts and buildings.

We went building by building looking for anything that would help our research. We found a lot of headstones with the name of Corvin on them. We also found names like Vasile and Dumitru. This was a very busy location with lots of families. It also had very detailed headstones and mausoleums. After a while we found a crypt that was opened, and we were able to make our way down into it. There were your normal slabs with bodies on them and nothing new anywhere in sight. This was a clear sign something was off since the door was open. Maybe another traveler had found this place and used it for shelter also, or maybe someone else was looking for answers like us.

Then we found what seemed to be a secret door that opened to a staircase that led into a deep dark hole. We found a torch and then had to find a way to light it. After a few minutes we found matches and lit the torch and started down the staircase. The stairs seemed to go forever but we kept tracking to see where it would lead. We finally reached the bottom and entered a room of coffins and urns. We looked around a bit and continued down a narrow hallway that led to more urns and coffins. The layer of dirt showed no one had been here in a long time and that leaves us not knowing who this vault belonged to and when or if they would return. The last room we found a small desk-like object with a letter on it. The writing appeared to be in blood and seemed very lengthy. We took a few minutes to read the letter and in it we found some answers we were searching for this whole time. The letter was left by another vampire and he spoke of the guilt he lived with and the regrets for what he had done in his life. He stated that all the urns were the people that were sacrificed so that he may live, and this was his way of paying respect to them. He wanted the world to know he wasn't a monster if this letter was ever found.

I placed the letter back on the table and we started looking for a place to sleep. During the search I found another door and as I entered the room, I found the skeleton of a man sitting in a chair staring at the wall. He was dressed in old garb and had the fangs of a vampire. He must have been the owner of this vault. The room had another small table with personal effects and an empty candelabra. There was also a chalice sitting on the table with blood stains running down it and wax holding it to the table. Other than these few things the room was empty and cold. He died alone and wanted to do so because of the guilt he carried. I have no way of knowing how old he was or when he turned. This clearly was an old crypt and he had been down to her a long time.

Chapter 20
The Journey Continues

The next evening we made our way back to the docks. We were going to head back to the states disappointed with the lack of information we turned up. I did discuss with Phillip about us going into business together. I was hoping I would not regret that decision later. Our plan was to sail back and take out every pirate ship on the way and use the bounty for paying for everything. It was easy to get information on what pirate ships were out there and what routes they followed.

The hardest part was getting close enough to the ships without them running. They would obviously see us from a distance so we would have to find a way to lure them onboard our boat in order to have the advantage. We also were not sure if we would even find any ships on our way back to the states luck would have to be on our side. Worst possible situation we make it home with less than we left with but that's a chance we will be taking.

We sailed for hours and then anchored when dawn was coming. Staying close enough to shore for the anchors to work made it hard because we didn't want to hit rocks or run aground in the shallows. The few hours of sleep we get will leave us vulnerable if anyone boards us, but we can't control that. That is the chance you take without mortal companions to travel with you. The next evening, we spent several hours heading towards home when through the mist we caught the site of another ship. We were hoping this was a pirate ship, so we locked the wheel towards the area of the ship and hid. We were hoping to be boarded and then we could take them out then transfer to their ship and take control of it.

As planned our ship was boarded and we slowly and quietly took out the borders. It did not take long for the others to figure out something was wrong. They sent more people and lights to try and figure out what was happening. Once the last group crossed over, we also crossed over and took command of the other ship. It was a bloody mess and we found it good to feed without worries. Then we crossed back over and cleared our ship of the pirates that were left. We kept a couple to use as food for the remaining journey home. They had a nice cell in the hull of their ship that we could utilize. The rest of the bodies we buried at sea. The important cargo we transferred to our ship then we split up and took the two ships towards home. We split the two ships up and travelled at a distance from one another so if another ship approached, we would have the advantage again of surprise.

I explain to Peter this is the beginning of what could be a very lucrative business partnership. Phillip and I became very close, almost like brothers. The startup took a while of course because we had to make contacts and buy businesses. We also had to find people we could trust to run things for us during the day. We of course worked all the night shifts and continued to build the business at a quick pace. Phillip took a while to settle in and start pulling his weight.

Chapter 21
Business As Usual

I poured myself completely into the business so I could stay busy and not think about the past and think about her. The plan after becoming successful was to expand back into our hometowns and rebuild our lives there. We built a very lucrative business and expanded where we could until he betrayed me which led us here.

I will spend one more night with Peter so I can prepare for my journey back home. I know what was going on here and at home must be connected but I did not know why. I still have work to do I am hoping of course it's Phillip so I can find him but whoever is behind this is covering their tracks well. Even if it is not Phillip, hopefully something about him still comes out during the search. Either way I need to fix this situation and stop it from happening again.

I return home and as soon as I hit the docks, I feel the presence hit me. I spend about an hour searching for the one I was sensing but they are one step ahead of me. After not being able to locate them, I head into town to try and locate the new vampires and a place to stay. I spend a couple hours but find no one or nothing to help me. I also can't find a suitable place to stay so I head back to my old flat.

I had visions as I slept of the past and I believe it is due to the fact I relieved it with Peter. I was reliving everything quickly until I saw Reina in the park. I ran across the field and just as I was about to grab her, she disappeared. I had this feeling of failing her all over again and when I went to call for her, I woke up and realize it was a dream. I couldn't sleep anymore, so I just wrote in my journal. I still have so much to do and cannot be distracted by my past, so I decide to head out into town once more.

I have two mysteries to solve and the only way to do so I feel is to hide in the shadows and just keep looking. Eventually something must happen to give me the leads I need. I spend the entire night travelling and sitting and find nothing but more frustration. I do not understand how or why they are avoiding me or if it is just a coincidence. I head back to the flat with thoughts of just giving up in my head but as I approach the door, I find a note taped to my door.

My first thought of course is who knows who I am and how did they know where I live? This of course makes me nervous because that means they can get me at my most vulnerable time. I really need a new place to stay until I figure this out. The note itself is interesting because inside is directions to where the coven of new vampires is located. There is also information on the number of vampires and a suggestion not to face them alone. The letter recommends following them and taking them one at a time.

The letter then takes a weird twist as the writer confesses to making the vampires and promises there will be no more. The explanation given was they got out of control before they could be properly train or be taught. The person writing shows remorse and sympathy for the young ones but could not kill them. The writer needs someone stronger and detached that can fix the problem. I also felt as if I recognize the writing, it was like someone I once knew. This left more questions and concerns that I did not need right now.

Chapter 22
A New Home

I can't focus on that. I must find a place to stay in the older part of town. This is where the vampires are held up and I need to work out a plan. I really need to assess the situation and see if it would be possible for me to handle it by myself. If they are as strong as the writer said they are, it could be a difficult task.

I know the old coffin maker lives in town, so I set out for his house. I thought he may let me stay with him for a little while. I could not think of another place but if he does not agree then I will have to look elsewhere. As I expect, the old shopkeeper is startled when he opens the door to find me standing there. He just gazes at me for a minute then asks what I need. He is much older and frail, he can barely get around. I explain to him that I need a room for a couple days and ask him if he will allow me to stay with him. He is hesitant to agree but finally did, then went on to ask why I appeared so young still. I then have to remind him of what I am. I also had to thank him for not telling anyone about me. Then I ask him to once again not to say anything to anyone about me being here.,

Now that I am settled in, I can go out to locate the hold up and all the members. The first one was easy to find because young vampires do not understand what they feel or how important it is to pay attention to what their senses are telling them. They also do not care if they draw attention to themselves. I follow him for a while from the shadows and assume I am good since he did not seem to notice me. Then out of the blue he stops and says stop following me and go home! I say nothing. I just stand still and wait to see what he is going to do next.

After a few minutes he starts looking around for me and talking out loud. He was saying how dare you come here and watch me without introducing yourself. It is time you come out and face me and explain why you are here. Stop hiding in the shadows and be a man. Just as I am about to go out three more come out of the shadows to join him. I am glad I waited because I would have been outnumbered and I am not sure how strong they are yet. I left the area without them seeing me with the plan of returning tomorrow.

I track down and follow a member of the coven back to their hideout to start this evening off. I stay in the shadows for a while and wait to make sure they were all inside. I feel based on what I saw that I will be able to take them with no help, but it might suit me better to try and work with them, so I have help in this area. I decide after a while to walk up and knock on the door and face them all at the same time. After I knock, I wait several minutes for someone to open the door. The young guy is like who are you and what the hell do you want? I say who I am does not matter but I need to see the leader of this coven. He says you are not going to see him or anyone else, leave before I make you regret coming here. I assure him that I am no threat and that he would be better off just doing as I ask.

After telling me to piss off he slams the door in my

face. I patiently waited there for a few minutes with hopes he went back and told someone else that would be curious about me. Then suddenly the door flies open and standing in the door is the alpha that I followed the other night. He is less than happy to see me and becomes aggressive quickly demanding to know why I was here and why I was in their business. I start to explain that I am observing their group to see what they were doing and explain that I can teach them the ways of our kind.

The leader interrupts me by laughing and saying how dare I come to his home and presume to think I can teach them anything. It is rude to assume we want someone to teach us and that I was going to die for sticking my nose in their business. I warned him that they would not be able to kill me, that they were much too young and much too weak. He began to laugh again saying that he is not worried and that he will show me who is weak. Then he instructs his crew to kill me. Within a couple minutes I have killed all of them except the alpha. I really want to get more information from him before killing him.

I then pin the alpha to a wall and explain that he has no chance to stop an elder. Then I ask him again about who had turned him and how long ago had he been turned. He wouldn't answer me at first, even though he knew he would die either way. Then as I was about to kill him, he looks at me and says a woman had turned him then vanished about a year ago. He said he created the rest of the pack after figuring out how to make more of their kind. Then he pleaded to live and join me.

I thought shortly of his pleas and explain to him that

if I was to let him live that he would need to be trained and would have to be loyal to me. I went over the basic rules and how we survive in the human world. He agreed out of self-preservation, but I know if his master returns, I will have to kill him. I told him to rest, and we will start rebuilding the pack as soon as we find suitable replacements. Then we will take over this city and run it together.

Chapter 23
A New Beginning

I left him at his safe house because I did not want him knowing too much about me yet and I must figure out who this woman is that had turned him. I did not know of any female vampires in the area, so this was very confusing. I must sleep and think about how to proceed even though he said he knew where to find more recruits. I hope they are quality people and not a bunch of useless fools like his last group.

As I sleep, she rushes my mind and disturbs me more and more. My mortal side still yearns for her, and I did not want to wake and lose her again. As I wake, I am hoping to see her and of course she is not there, and I do not understand where these thoughts of her come from. I know she is gone, and I will never hear from her again but I still long for her touch. I got a strange feeling about her but cannot say exactly what I am feeling but it is something strong.

I sit and think a while before heading out and must refocus on the task at hand. I have to fix the problems in this area before continuing my journey looking for the one responsible for this and clues to Phillips' new home. I have a lengthy meeting with the alpha and we discuss the future here. I also try to get more information but there is no more. It is a waste of time to try, my best bet is just sitting up things here and moving on to other areas.

I head down toward the docks after another short

meeting so I can gather my thoughts. I am a block or so from the docks when the presence returns from before. I know it must be her and she has to be watching me, but I don't know why she has not made contact thus far. I stop and yell out for her to join me so we can talk and end this game. I wait several minutes with no response. I then continue down to the docks. The presence as usual vanishes leaving me alone.

I find my spirits down and vampires are not to carry mortal feelings. My thirst for blood though has not replaced my love for her. I will never be happy in this life if I can't let go of her. I am about to leave when Peter shows up with news that they found information on Phillip and his operations. I ask him if the information is accurate and how soon he would be able to leave. Then I ask if he was going to go with me on this leg of my journey. He says he will be ready and have everything set up by the next evening.

Peter informed me it will take two days to reach the town Phillip is said to be in. The chances of finding him are not to my favor but it was worth going there. If I find Phillip, then my work would just be starting because I have so many business-related things to catch up on. I was not sure what to expect upon arrival, but I did tell Peter I wanted to face Phillip alone in case things went wrong. He agrees and the plan was for me to contact him when it was done if I survive.

Two days and this could all be over and then I can go back and finish researching the female vampire. She is causing a lot of trouble and does not realize the damage she is causing. I need to stop her and keep more vampires from being made. She says she understands but I am not fully convinced.

Chapter 24
The Hunt

The end of the second day is here as we approach the harbor. That is my signal to hide below and try to blend in and not be detected in case Phillip is there. He is not expecting me because he believes I am gone but I do not want to take chances. I do have second thoughts about killing him, but it is the only way to finish this whole thing.

I am not familiar with the area, but I know Phillip and I figure tracking him through his habits should be easy. He is really into night life unlike me who does not want to bring attention to myself. I know he also likes to sit up high and watch the city in the way a bird of prey will do in the wild. With that in place, leaving the ship is more dangerous and I must be extremely careful not to let my presence known.

We left the ship with no issues and looked for shelter to hold up in while we are in town. Sleeping during the day is what we do but it seems the closer to the past I get the more it seems to haunt me with her memories. I do not know why I am still longing to be with her, but I just can't seem to leave her behind. I am beginning to think there is a reason she will not leave my dreams. Time will tell but until then I must stay focused on tracking down Phillip it is harder than I expected. There are no signs of him, and a few people have stories of someone who could have been him but nothing to say for sure. Now it is the third frustrating day and I tell Peter we should leave the next night since nothing has turned up that we can use.

I awoke to a familiar presence near me. I am not sure if he feels me, but I am fully aware of him. It appears my ambition has paid off. I am finally going to face Phillip. I quickly make my way to the street and there passing by is Phillip, he stops and looks around as if someone has smacked him on the back of the head. Then our eyes lock, and he gives me this smirk like he just got away with something. He starts to speak but I grab him before he can get it out. I toss him into the shadows and all the years of torment and hell. The being buried alive comes out of me all at once. I tear him apart, but he isn't dead yet and I feel the need to tell him what I felt and that I am taking everything back that he stole.

He starts to crawl away, but he has been weakened and is not able to go very fast. I start laughing and quickly reach down and tear his head off his body. Then I just sit back and look at what I have just done. I feel I have accomplished my mission, but I still feel empty and unfulfilled. I vow now he will be the last person I let do me like that. It all happened so fast I didn't get to enjoy it or make him suffer like I wanted to. I gathered up his body and look for a place to give him a proper burning to ensure he will never return like I was able to.

Lucky for me he had documents on him that led me to his place when I searched his clothes. This gave me a more permanent shelter so I can stay here for a while. Peter said he would be leaving the next evening and so we made the arrangements to make sure he left with no problems. I explain that I need to stay until I get things taken care of here and it seems that it will be an easy transition since Phillip has everything so well organized and laid out in his office.

Chapter 25
The Takeback Begins

P eter left for the ship and I am going to meet him to see him off but I stay behind instead to continue going through things in the office. I have time to kill so I start with some old books sifting through them looking for anything that would help, but instead I find two very weird, old pictures. The first picture is of Peter and Philip together and the second is of me and my wife together. This made no sense to me but hopefully Peter has an explanation as to why Phillip has these pictures. I gathered a few things and head out to meet up with Peter.

I arrive at the meeting place, but Peter is nowhere to be found. I did find it strange that he is not there, but I figure he found something to get into and would turn up. I just sat and thought about the next move I will make. The next logical thing would be to track down the lawyer in charge of the business affairs. I assume that I am still on everything since there would be no record of my death. He would need that to take me off everything and so I should be able to simply regain control no questions asked.

The lawyer was easy to track down because the name is the same as when I left. So, either this is a descendant or Phillip turned our Lawyer into a vampire so he wouldn't have to find a new one. It took a couple days, but I finally have a meeting with the lawyer and have a chance to start looking into things. He is acting weird, and I am not sure I can trust him. I am not sure how much he knows or how involved he is with things. I must give it a few days and test him. I explain to him that Phillip would not be returning to the business and asks if there was a way to legally remove him without his signature or death certificate. Then he asks me if I killed him out of revenge since he had stolen the businesses from me and left town. Then he showed that he knew we were vampires and that he did not want any trouble.

I ask him if he wants to stay on and continue his role and if so then I need full disclosure of everything. He agrees and we spent several days going through paperwork and financials for all the businesses currently in operation. We also look to see if there is a way to expand or increase profits on any parts of the business. Then the next step is for me to meet all the operational managers and bookkeepers for each division of the business.

After several days I realize all was going well here but that I have not heard from Peter. I decide to go looking for him in hopes of getting some answers and ensuring he is safe. I check his hotel and the docks and find nothing. He is gone without a trace. Now I am curious about what he is hiding. Eventually I will find him, and he will answer my questions but until then I have business to deal with. With the end of the week approaching, I know I need to stay for at least another week. My plan is to finish up here and transfer what I can back home. I am hoping the lawyer is interested in transferring also once everything is settled.

While going through some final documents I find a

list of properties. Each one in a different place, and I am confused about it, so I go to the lawyer to inquire about them. He informs me that the properties are halfway houses of sorts for new vampires or for travelling vampires. He says Phillip did his best to take care of those in need of assistance, even though he was a less than desirable person. I decide I need to travel to each location and then sell or restructure the properties to fit my plans. I will need someone to manage the properties. I will have the lawyer locate someone to handle this part of the business, since Phillip is no longer here to deal with them.

As much as I have grown to hate Phillip, he really has put a lot of care into taking care of our business and of others like us. The lawyer wants to stay here and run operations. He did not feel uprooting would help fix anything and so after much conversation I agree. I am going to leave at the end of the second week. I will make the journey to research all our properties and decide the best plan moving forward. I make the lawyer partner and give him full power of attorney and a better salary from the business income. I am putting a lot of trust in him, but he also knows what crossing me will cause so I feel it was a good gamble.

Chapter 26
New Business

I set out on my journey and I can hit the two closest properties first. My search turns up nothing and it seems as if no one had been in these places for a long time. The third property was intriguing due to mine and Philips things are inside it. It also has my wife's things stored inside. I am upset that her things are here, and I am also confused. I stood there in deep thought, and without warning I am thrown across the room and I quickly bounce back. I was so lost in thought I didn't sense the presence there with me.

We struggle for a few minutes, and I end up pinning him to the wall. Then I demand that he tell me who he is and why he is here. He replies saying this is his masters house and that he is not allowed to let anyone access or stay in the house. I then explain to him that his master is dead and that I am in charge now, that I am the new master. I also ask if he lives here and what his intentions are now that Phillip is no more. He is unsure even after I explained why Phillip had to die.

He agrees to stay and follow my lead, and he says he did not know who the woman is I had asked him about. He explains that he oversees most of the properties and has contact with the ones he did not. I explain to him my plans and that he could stay in charge until I needed him elsewhere. I also ask him if he recalls a vampire by the name of Peter and he told me Peter has been there on a regular basis with Phillip. They seemed to be good friends and business associates.

I spent the next few weeks researching the properties and gathering information. I continued to find clues of Peter and the confusion I had was building. I needed to find Peter and get answers, and I also figure he knew Phillip and that is how he knew where to find him. He set Phillip up and lied to me without reason. I need to settle things and finish this quickly. My next journey was to Peter's house, that's the only place left to search.

I arrived at Peters to find it abandoned and dusty. It seems as if no one has been here in a while and all signs of Peter are gone. I check his main house and all the sheds and guest houses on the property. The last place I find is an underground crypt. Even though I was already confused, what I found in the crypt was worse. I found the clothes my wife had been wearing the night she disappeared. I just stood there looking for a moment then realize I had no idea what had really happened since she was taken. I start to really question how long Peter and Phillip has been working together.

I gather her things and I continued with my journey leaving Peters with more questions than answers. I continue looking for clues of Peter just the same as I did Phillip. The difference was Peter stayed to himself and never drew attention to himself. This will make it hard to track him down. I now believe Peter may be the key to everything and he may have overseen all of it. I have so much on my mind as I made my way back to the dock. Then out of nowhere I feel the familiar presence upon me and as I have done in the past I call out for an answer. I make it clear I am done with the games but as usual there is no answer and no one coming out. Then as quickly as it came it left. Leaving frustration and more questions which is not why I came here but that is what I am leaving with yet again.

Chapter 27
The Trap

I decide leaving here is a bad idea and that I need to trap her. I assume the presence is the female I have been told about. I need help and that is what I am going to work on next. I will gather up all the vampires in the area I can that will help me and just hope that they are not children of hers. The plan must be great because she is always one step ahead of me and I need to end this.

My plan is to meet the next evening and execute the plan to capture her. I do not know what will happen, but I need to be ready for whatever happens. I head back to Peter's to rest and before I realize it I was lost in thought looking at her clothes. I wonder if she suffered and where she ended up. I wonder where her body ended up and if she got buried. I wonder if she was brought here and if she is still here somewhere. I may never know what happened, but I will keep looking until I find Peter or the answers I am looking for.

The time is now to put my plan into action by sweeping the city back towards the dock. I chose the dock because that is where she is always at when I notice her. I went straight down the main road and the guys flanked me so we could cover more ground and hope to circle around her. She always seems to be just outside the perimeter and hopefully this time we catch her slipping up. I wonder if it is just weird timing that I always find her or just coincidence. The other option is she plans it this way on purpose . After a while I figure it is done and I send everyone on their way. She is not coming; we have not found anything again.

I walk back towards the house and my mind is racing about everything that has happened until this point. I am deep in thought and not paying attention to my surroundings. I think there is no danger since the presence never showed up. I was mistaken because I am grabbed out of nowhere by 8 big vampires who left me with a warning. They inform me their master demands that I stop looking for the girl or they will be back to kill me. Then as quickly as they showed up, they are gone. Leaving me even more questions about the girl, which is now confirmed and who is their master.

This group has no idea who I am, or they would have tried to just finish me now. Whoever sent them should know that I will not stop until I find the answers I seek. I will confront this master one day face to face and I will also meet this mysterious woman. It is just a matter of time and one day it will not seem like I am just meant to suffer. It is exciting to know my life is never dull but at the same time I am ready to just live without all these constant problems happening.

I decide to sweep the docks again by myself and I take my time hoping to draw her out. I walk for hours calling out, but nothing happens. I realize this person just does not want anything to do with me and maybe it is just all a coincidence but how did they know I was looking for her. Someone must be working with both of us, and I need to be extra careful moving forward.

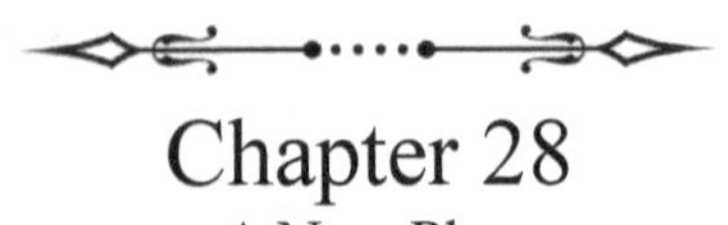

Chapter 28
A New Plan

My next step is to turn the business over to the lawyer and just collect a commission. This way I do not have any anchors or concerns keeping me distracted. I will just let the lawyer run everything with our associates and that will allow me to travel and research everything that is happening. I know I do not have to worry about him crossing me, so I set out to Peter's place once again hoping to make contact with him. There is nothing here and I still have no answers. I don't find him, and I realize I have spent my time as a vampire looking for answers and I keep coming up empty. I make the decision to only focus on living, leaving my past behind me. I will travel for the next few years finding new cities and groups of vampires. I find that the rules I thought I knew for our kind were not followed by all and that may be why Phillip was not punished for my death. The only rules that seem to matter are the ones taught to you by the one who make you. Then later it becomes about self-preservation. I did find that the longer I travel and embrace my life the more of my mortality I lost.

The more I focused on my life now the more I enjoyed the hunt and the more the dark side of me took over my being. The more I change the more at peace I feel and the more in control I seem to be in. I now enjoy the night and all that comes with it and the freedom of not looking over my shoulder or feeling some weird people following me. I finally realize that Phillip was right about just giving into my animalistic cravings and start really living as a vampire in complete control of the night. No more human limitations will hold me back and I can let her and everyone else behind for good.

I find what living really is with all my new friends I meet on my journey. I am also able to get involved in more business ventures and continue to build my wealth. The want for power and money start controlling me the same way it controlled Phillip. I also did my best to unite as many groups of vampires as possible. The more teamwork we build the better business will run and the better preservation of the species we will have.

Several years into my travels I end up back home and I am not even thinking about my past popping back up. I have moved past it all. My only reason for coming back here is to unite all my businesses and tie up loose ends. I know I can make a name for myself and even get the recognition of other elder vampires. My next trip will be to London where I will be able to expand overseas. This will allow me real power in two countries and make tons of money.

The only problem with travelling by boat to get overseas is the vulnerability while you are sleeping. You can't control anything from down below the ship or during the daytime hours. You must worry about pirates, storms and floating off course and ending somewhere you do not want to end up. The only way to prevent that is to travel with people and hope they do not turn on you.

Chapter 29
Off Course

I was not able to secure a ride with someone else, so I will take a ship and head out on my own. I miss the crew I originally travelled with but they are gone and finding a new crew is even harder than before. I find an empty ship and leave the docks early in the evening. The ship did what I did not want, it floated off course and I end up somewhere very south of where I need to be. Lucky for me I am resourceful and have the means to track the countryside wherever I land. It will take several days to get back on track but that is where the adventure comes into the trip. This was the case of course when Phillip and I were tracking Dracula all those years ago.

The first step is finding exactly where I am so I can plan my trip to London. This will be time consuming, but I have no one waiting for me which means I am not on a schedule. I make my way from the ship into the forest in front of me not knowing when I would find civilization. The only noise I heard for hours was nature and the occasional boat horn from the coast. I was a few hours into my journey when out of nowhere the presence that had haunted me all those years ago makes itself known and startles me. I do not want to let her know I feel her presence, so I just ignore it and keep walking. Eventually the presence disappears, and it makes me wonder if she was following me or if because I am so strong now, I can just sense her.

I have walked for hours with nothing turning up and no sounds except the forest. With daylight approaching I need to find shelter from the daylight but there is nothing around so I will have to return to the ground. I found a thick brush area and dug in underneath it, and unlike the last time I was in the ground I will rise this time. The night is mine now and I will never be kept from it again.

This evening was more of the same. I just walk for hours searching for a town or a camp where I can feed and hopefully find out where I am. I am not finding anything, no graveyards or farms. There are no campsites or caves I can look through. There is just nothing, so I just keep following my compass north. I was really in it this time I was completely on my own and as I walk a fog moves in and the temperature changes. I at this point wish I could fly like older vampires are said to have the power to do.

Today I must dig into the ground again to hide from the daylight. I do not seem to be making much progress and I am starting to get thirsty. I really need to find something soon. I move on still following my compass, I find what appears to be an abandoned town. Time has forgotten this place and you can tell there had not been life here in a long time. Everything is covered in dirt and all the windows are busted out. Nature has overgrown this town and completely taken over. I spend a few hours looking through the building and find nothing.

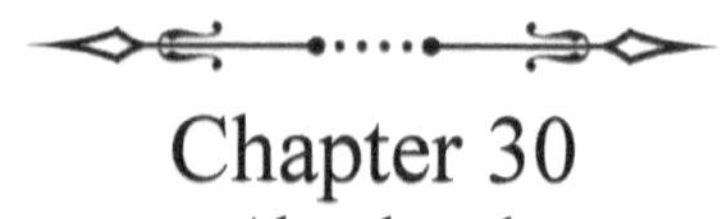

Chapter 30
Abandoned

I have spent several days searching for something and left empty handed. The town provided shelter for me, and I hate to leave but I need to feed and continue looking for business opportunities. Lucky for me even though I woke early there is a heavy overcast and I am protected. I start walking out the north side of the town when I see a weird path leading into another part of the forest. The curious side of me wins out and I follow the path to the end of it. What I find is disturbing even for me. It is an old cemetery that has been destroyed. Graves dug up and tombstones broken and scattered. Skeletons lay everywhere and all the tomb doors have been broken and removed. It is clear someone or something destroyed everything here looking for something or someone.

It is very uncommon for vampires to disrespect the dead like this, and it adds a complexity to the question of what exactly happened here and in town. I decide to spend the day going through the tombs and researching what might have happened here. I find no clues but did find a good place to rest for the day. This did make me realize that Peter and vampires like him are out there and that I may have to find one again to prevent something like this from happening again.

I spent the next four days trekking through the countryside and forest before finding a small town. I find an old man walking down a street by himself late at night and I took him without care. I need to feed, and he would hold me over until I can figure out where I am. In the past I would have found another way to feed but the new me has no concerns about human life or the consequences of my actions. I finally figure out where I was after a little research. I find myself in a village just outside the town of Ars.

This makes me a long way from London and in the middle of a country that has a heavy French and Spanish influence. The country I was in is Andorra and this place is beautiful. It reminds me a lot of home with Architecture. The color pallet and the organization of the city is amazing and may be a great place to set up an outpost.

The houses are made of brick and layered to add beauty and strength. The rooms from the outside seem to be big and ready for large gatherings. The houses are tucked in the base of the mountain, and all have statues made of stone. They appear to be of an older society and religion. You can tell the influence of this area has many different cultures. I do not know or understand the main language of Catalan but it does not appear I will be hearing it anyway.

This town will make a good place for a large population or a headquarters for a business. I know a little about the area and spent some time on the coast, so I am not completely lost here. I would much prefer to be in Barcelona or Catalonia but this is not too far from either. I just hope when I clear the mountains there will be traces of life.

It seems the farther I run from my past the more it smacks me in the face. You can't live this long and not face everything you have been through. The main thing is to keep moving forward and do not let the memories distract you from the journey. I hope to hit the coast and find passage to London and leave this behind me. I may not live beyond facing Peter but today my only worry is finding him.

I realize I am pushing myself like I did with Phillip. I am allowing my life to be controlled by wanting revenge for someone who had wronged me. I realize I need to slow down and enjoy the country I find myself in, of course if I had found safe passage to London I would not be here. Hindsight is twenty- twenty and I sure wish we had foresight so we did not make the mistakes that we do. My future is not written so I must be vigilant and move with purpose.

Chapter 31
Transportation Arranged

I spent a couple weeks just enjoying myself until I came to the city of Pic Du Port in France. This is a thriving place and with plenty of travelers it can make a great business out post. It also offers plenty of opportunities to feed for vampires. Unfortunately, if you are not set up here there is no shelter so I will have to travel in and out of town until I find passage out of port.

By the fourth week I was able to find a boat that travels to the United Kingdom. I need to be on that boat, so I decide to contact the ship's captain, the plan is to let them in on my secret. They will see I want to trust them. I will need to barter with them, so the relationship is beneficial to both sides. If for some reason things don't go as planned, I will have to kill them and take the boat.

I hope it does not come to that because finding a crew for the daytime is challenging. With that in mind I follow the crew to an old-world style pub. I think meeting them in a non-threatening situation will make things easier. The pub is old, and everything is made of heavy thick wood from the floor to the rafters. The pub seems to be family operated and there are only a couple of people working. There is the old man behind the bar and the middle-aged woman serving the crowd. The crowd is diverse and seems as though the wrong thing said, or the wrong thing done will cause a major brawl.

The ale is warm and has things floating in it. This ale was not filtered or strained before it was kegged and sent out. The whiskey and scotch appear the same and makes me believe the stuff is probably made in house. I would guess most places here will be the same. I chose not to partake at this place, but I might end up doing so if I am going to get close to the crew.

I order a round of ales and head over to the crew. I set the glasses down and then ask who the captain is. I figure the older guy across the room in the group of older sailors. To my surprise a young man stands up and claims to be the captain. He then asks me what business I have with him and his crew. He also said I am stupid to think it is ok to interrupt their down time. He is sincerely not a likeable person at first approach.

I reply to him that I do not mean any disrespect and that I am just looking to have a business conversation. I explain I bought these drinks as a sign of peace and respect and will just need a minute of their time. He then says fine but make it quick and you better not be wasting my time. I assure him that I am not and give them a quick outline of what I was in search of. I then tell them we will need to meet on the ship so I can give them the rest of the information. I also explain I want to check out the ship to make sure it will work for what I need.

The captain says they will meet me on the ship, and he wants to know in detail what his crew will get out of this deal. I explain to the captain that he and the crew will be paid very well and that all my business would go through them alone. I tell them that helping me will guarantee them income no matter the season. The captain tells me that he and his men will need to discuss things but will meet me at the boat later. Then they will allow me to look at the boat if they decide to work with me.

Later that night I meet the crew on the ship as agreed upon. They agree to work with me and give me the opportunity to search the boat top to bottom. I then gather the captain and crew on the deck of the ship. I then explain to them that I am a vampire and I need safe passage. I explain that I can't come out in the day, and I am not safe travelling on my own long distances. I explain that I need a crew willing to assist me. I also mention that I am in search of someone but cannot accomplish this on my own.

I then tell them the reason I need the right ship is because I need to carry a coffin onboard that I can leave for when I am onboard. I also make them understand this ship is the only one that travels where I need to go and that I really need them to be onboard. I then make it clear that if they do not believe me and do not want to help me then I will take their ship and build a new crew by force. Then I leave to give them a day to really think about the situation and what path they want to go. Now that we are back together, I ask what their decision is. One of the crew members starts to laugh and says this crazy asshole is pulling our leg. We should just throw his ass off the ship and call a doctor to help him. To make all of them understand I am not crazy but extremely serious I quickly snatch him up off the ground and show him my fangs and the glow of my eyes. Then to scare him I levitate up over the ship and throw him. Just before he hits the water, I grab him and pull him back on deck. This of course completely drains me, but I cannot let them know that. I believe I am still evolving and one day this will not bother me.

The whole crew is shocked and backs up from me. I explain to them they do not have to be afraid unless they cross me. I promise them that the crew will always be safe if I am onboard. I can only come out at night and that during the daytime I wouldn't bother them. I made it clear I need day walkers I can trust and that I hope they will agree to work with me. I say farewell and tell them I will return the next evening to get their final answer.

Chapter 32
No Games

When I return I decide to watch from afar to see what they are up to. I figure one of three things will happen. The first would be they have already left or are getting ready to so they can avoid me. The second is they contacted the local authorities to have me ambushed. The last thing is they are waiting to tell me they are interested in working together which will be best for everyone.

After watching for a few minutes, I realize they are trying to leave before I arrive. Trying to scare them did not work so I must approach it differently. I go down and get on the ship without them noticing. I hide below deck so I will be safe from the sun. I will not have my coffin, but I can find somewhere to sleep. I plan on staying here until we are at sea and the crew is separated from the captain.

About an hour after setting sail, I make my way to the dining area. It is a room with a couple tables and cards and rum spread throughout the room. It is smoke filled from cigars and cigarettes. I watch for a while and once I feel enough of the crew members are in the room I shut and secure the door from the outside. This will give me far less issues dealing directly with the captain and figuring out what to do next.

I make my way on deck and find the captain at the wheel. I sit down behind him without him noticing me here. I wait until he starts yelling for his crew then I stand directly behind him. When he turns to walk towards the door, I am there face to face with him. He falls backward and lands on the deck. Then in a scared voice he asks where his crew is and if they are still alive.

I grab him up off the floor and say you left the bay without me. I told you; no one would get hurt if you just gave me a straight answer. Now your crew is dead, and you are next. How quickly do you want to die? In a scared voice he starts pleading for his life. Please don't kill me he says, I will do whatever you want just don't kill me. I stare at him then drop him to the deck. He then asks me how I killed his crew and why since they did nothing wrong. They just followed orders from their captain. The crew has families and people relying on them to make it back home. He says how can I run a ship without them. I then explain that he has killed his crew by not following my orders.

He then pleads again for me to spare him and that even though I was clearly a monster that he will do whatever I need. I smile and tell him that we have a deal then and that he needs to remember how easy it is for me to remove them without anyone knowing. He continues to agree and beg for mercy. I say very well you may live. Then I tell him our first piece of business will be releasing his crew from the dining facility and the second would be to get me a coffin.

He looks at me with disbelief and runs off to find his crew. When he and the crew return, I ask if they all now understand how easily I can get rid of them but that is not my goal. I just want safe passage to ports and that is all. I would like to have a standing relationship and pay your crew for all my travels. I do not wish to harm you at all. I throw a bag of coins and gems at the captain to split among him and the crew. I make it clear that I will not interfere with their business if they do not interfere with mine. Then I head to the bottom of the ship to find safety from the approaching day.

Chapter 33
England Town

The next evening I walk out on deck as the lights of what appears to be an English town is coming into sight. I smile knowing it was a quick trip and that the crew is behind me. Before leaving the ship, the captain approaches me and informs me that he and the crew have had a long meeting and that they will be working with me and providing whatever help I need.

I just stare at the crew as they leave the ship. As the last crew member leaves, I feel the presence of another vampire appear. The presence seems close, and I still have no idea who is around and if they are following me. I can only assume this vampire is seeking a meal. I leave the ship and head toward town. I need to find a place to camp until I figure out my next plan of my journey.

The walk down the road is perplexing to me with the amount of people on the streets and the amount of vampires present. You would think that the vampires or the humans would be hiding at this time of the day. The vampires here must be young and do not fear themselves being found out. I can only assume I have found a coven of vampires and they must have a strong hold here in one of the buildings.

Covens in Europe have been around for centuries and only in the United States do vampires seem to thrive on their own with maybe one partner. Interested in knowing more I pick up the trail of a female and start following her back through town. After a while I realize we are being followed and that she has not detected me. I assume she has not learned to detect others yet. I circle back to try and locate who is following us. What I find is a group heading in the same direction. This means I am going in the right direction, and I will hopefully meet the coven leader.

I follow them to the edge of town to an old warehouse. It appears to be abandoned and nothing like the coven building I have read about. Maybe this is a makeshift set up and they are still looking for a permanent set up. I do not have time to head back into town so when the area is cleared, I follow them into a set of cellar doors. I have no idea what I will find but I need to get inside.

I walk down the stairs until I come to where it splits into two halls. I decide to follow the hall with the strongest presence. This hall leads through several doorways into a main room. Here I find candles lit and several caskets line the walls. I make my way towards another door where suddenly four of them were on top of me, before I can react to feeling their presence. Out of self-preservation I have no choice but to destroy all four of them. They did not give me a chance to talk or explain why I am here; they just wanted to kill me.

I stand over their bodies feeling bad for what I have done when a strong presence comes in behind me. I feel him move towards me so without a word I turn and grab him by the throat and lift him off the ground. I ask him if he is the coven leader, and he shakes his head yes. Then he says you killed four of my children and you will die for this, I tell him he is too weak and not able to threaten anyone. If you want the rest to live, you will listen to me closely. I am here only seeking to talk to you and find shelter for the day. I have no intentions of hurting anyone, but they attacked me, and I must defend myself.

I continue to explain like him they are all young and weak and untrained. I could easily have killed all of you on the street as I followed you back here, but I was only seeking shelter. I ask him if I let you live will you help me and give me answers to questions that I have. He shakes his head yes again, but I can tell he just wants to kill me. I set him down and tell him to sit down so we can talk.

I begin to question him about who had turned him and how many has he turned since. How many are in this group and how much was he told about being a vampire. I kept my eyes on him because he seems ready to strike out. I re-enforce the fact that I am on a journey of revenge and to get back what I lost, and that this is a small stop on my journey. I do not want to hurt anymore of your people but maybe I can help them.

He smiles and says they will be just fine on their own and don't need help from a stranger that knows nothing about them. A woman vampire has turned him into this and then disappeared. He only makes the others, so he is not alone. He explains it took several tries to figure out how and that he lost his best friend in the process. They feed off the docks and leave the townspeople alone since most of them are friends and family.

He then tells me another guy has come through just like me for the day. He had shown him how to complete the turning without killing the person and helped them set up the coven. He too then disappeared. The guy he describes sounds like Peter, and I know I am on the right track. I offer to stay a few days and help them with more training. He declines and says he expects me to be gone by dusk. I agree and he shows me a place I can sleep. I sleep very lightly for fear they will attack me when I cannot defend myself.

The evening comes and I meet with the coven. I thank them for allowing me rest and I apologize again for having to kill several of them. I then explain to them the importance of learning to sense other vampires and how powerful they are before trying to attack them. Vampires like me have been around hundreds of years and have powers you have not yet begun to tap into. I tell them they have a long journey ahead of them and I left as I had promised.

Chapter 34
On The Trail

I head north out of town figuring this is the way Peter would have gone. I also figure I will find more covens along the way and more evidence of the mystery lady. I have no idea what the path ahead of me holds but I must be ready for anything and keep moving forward. I just hope I can make this journey a short one. I am tired of chasing the past.

I find the next town very quickly and the presence of vampires have all but disappeared. This is good for me less chances of a confrontation and a better chance of finding a meal along the way. I do miss the days of feeding briefly but this journey has weakened me and made me more dependent. Once this trip is over, I will be dead or completely at ease and this stress will be no more.

I find what appears to be an abandoned building just before daybreak. The building is dirty and has not been used in years based on the appearance. I find a small room with no windows and just one entrance, so I settle in there for the day. I shut the door and start clearing a spot for me on a table. Then suddenly the door flies open, and someone grabs me. He then begins yelling and asking what the hell am I doing in his uncle's shop.

I grab him back and push him up against a wall. I snarl and my fangs show white and bright. I can smell his blood and feel his heartbeat raise as he is in shock. I can tell he did not know what I was at first and I want to drink his blood so bad. Then just before biting into his neck I think this could be a missed opportunity. I sit him back down on the floor and back up. I slam the door to block the light and then begin to speak.

I say to him I just need a place to sleep for the day and that I will be leaving in the dark. I do not mean any harm. I thought the building was abandoned and would provide good shelter. He just stood there looking at me and I can see his wheels turning. He sat down and passed out from the shock of what just happened. I picked him up and sit him in a chair instead of leaving him on the floor.

I wait several minutes for him to wake up, and then I shake him. He jumps to his feet and runs for the door. I grab him and put him back in the chair and tell him to relax. I explain if I wanted to harm him it would have already happened. I say again I just need shelter for the day and if he wants, I will pay him. I also ask him what kind of business this is, and would he be interested in firing it back up again if I finance it.

We sit there for several minutes then he says that he had not seen a vampire since his uncle was killed by one a year ago, and that he thought all vampires just wanted to kill humans. He says he got lucky that daylight was upon them, and he managed to escape outside before the vampire could kill him. It was the worst thing he had ever experienced, and the vampire was completely heartless.

He says he only escaped because his uncle had run a wooden stick through the vampire's heart and that his uncle died about an hour later. He then describes how he disposed of the vampire's body burning it in a wood pile outside. He then closed the shop and only comes back time to time, to check on things. I apologize to him and explain that not all vampires are like that and usually the younger the vampire the more out of control they are. I then tell him the importance of having human friends or acquaintances in order to run a business so we can thrive. We can't do business meetings during the day, and we can't operate during the day so we need someone we can trust to partner with us.

His name is Max and I tell him I will finance the rebuilding of this business if he just allows me a place to stay when I am in town. I tell him I would also need to trust him fully for this to work. I cannot bring back his uncle, but I can help him on his journey if he allows me to. He says he would need to think it over and he left. He agrees to let me stay for the day but then I must leave. I sit here and think things out, I know I cannot trust him, and he probably will come back and try to kill me in my sleep.

I have a few minutes left before the sun comes up all the way, so I search quickly for another place to hide. He appears to be gone so I want another place that will allow me to hear him if he returns. I find a small door that leads into what seems to be an old office or storage area. I can go in there and move things around to make a suitable place to sleep. This will also make him think I have left if he returns to the office.

I lay there all day but barely sleep. I am too anxious. I know where I go next will allow me to sleep. I just need to make it through today. He never returned as night falls upon me. It is time to move on, so I go down to the floor where I had come into the building. I open the door to leave, and Max is standing there as he is about to come into the building.

We stand here for a minute staring at each other, before Max says he needs to talk. The first thing he says is he does not trust me or the situation, but he feels as if he really does not have a choice but to work with me. He then asks exactly what I need from him and how long I will be here. I then explain that I just need a safe place to sleep and hold up until I finish some business I have here in town. I also will need help from him to do research into a man named Peter.

He probably has businesses or contacts in the area. I figure once we get everything, I will help him get his family business up and running. I also tell him I will try to make sure there are no more vampires made. We spend the rest of the evening talking business and I tell my story and why I am here. I try to make him understand normal vampires try to avoid humans. I also apologize for what happened to his family. I agreed to give him more information and we can strategies later.

The next evening Max returns with the news I need; he has found evidence that Peter was only a day's walk away from us. He is tied to several businesses, and they all were ones that operated late at night. Bars, restaurants and Burlesque shows. Some of them are open all day so it's possible to hide there and not worry about the daylight.

I thank him and say he has kept his end of the bargain and so I was going to keep mine. I hand him a bag of cash and tell him I will continue to send funds until he has levelled out. I also explain that if things go as planned that I will want him to take over the businesses I was going to acquire. You can tell he just realized this deal will make him wealthy. He is happy about that and agrees to help.

Chapter 35
Closing In

Peter has no idea I am on his trail and I should be able to find him. I know when I get in range, he will be able to sense my presence. That is the only thing that will possibly mess up my plan. I only have the name of the businesses, so I am hoping that I can locate them and him quickly. Best case I catch him walking to work so we are not in public view.

I acquire a horse to make the trip go faster but even with those the same old story plaques me. The problem of daylight approaching and the need for protection. Part of me wants to just say to hell with it and just burn up and end all of this. The other part of me does not want to give Peter and Phillip the satisfaction. I ride until nearly sunrise when I come across what appears to be an old family cemetery with a lot of vaults.

I approach the graveyard slowly thinking I can find an open vault or shed I can hold up in for the day. As I cross the fence line the presence of another vampire hits me. I move slowly and quietly so I will not spook whoever it is. I am in a strange place and at a disadvantage. I want to avoid a confrontation, so I move slowly around the perimeter until I find a shed and I slip in without running into anyone.

When I awake, I leave the shed and there waiting for me is four male and three female vampires. Well, most seem like vampires the rest are humans. I do not show them that I am startled, and I just stare them down. The one that seems to be the alpha steps forward and states I have a couple minutes to explain why I was trespassing before they remove me.

I then tell him that I am on my way to the city and did not want any trouble. I just needed a safe place to rest and that I am leaving now. He laughs and stares at his group; I can tell he was showing off. He then says I can leave only if he allows me too. I make it clear to him that none of them are strong enough to stop me.

He starts laughing and takes a step toward me, I quickly grab him and one other of the males and jump straight up in the air. I then tell him if he wants to live and protect his group it is best for him not to stand in my way. Then I let go of the other guy and go back to the ground. I land and catch the guy just before he hits the ground.

I let both go and step back. The group backs up and starts to run. I ask the alpha about Peter before he can disappear. He says they have never met Peter and that the vampire that had turned them is a woman. She vanished shortly after they were turned. They have not seen any other vampires until now.

I ask what the female looked like and how long ago it was that she was here. The description he gave made me pause for a second because the description sounds like Reina. She was dead so this is a weird coincidence, and I cannot put much into it. The time frame was not that long ago so that did not fit either. I then ask if he knew of any other vampires in the area. He says there is not and that if there was, they have not seen or heard of them.

I say thank you and suggest in the future you should

know who you're dealing with instead of trying to impress someone. Being the alpha means you must be the leader and protector. Learn the difference between a threat and someone clearly just passing through. Then I make my way to where I left the horse. When I get there the horse is gone so I head out on foot.

Once again as I walk, I find myself lost in thoughts of her. I know she must be dead but hearing him describe the woman is just too much. I realize I will never be over her if something as simple as a description does this to me. Was it possible though, is Reina a vampire and not dead after all. If so, why would she not just come to me.

I am not watching time, but I figure I will be in town before the sunrise. I know whatever the truth is I need to stop thinking about it until after I deal with Peter because it can cause me to make mistakes. I start focusing once again when I hit the city and see how big it is and how many people are here. There is no sense of vampires in the area, just humans. I need to scope out the place and find where Peter's businesses are.

I start investigating the outer perimeter businesses and worked my way towards the burlesque club which is dead center of the city. I can find shelter at one of the abandoned buildings and I will continue the next evening. Everywhere I go and everyone I talk to I come up with the same answer. No one knows or has ever seen Peter; they all have been hired by managers at the locations or by a business partner of Peters.

I got the information I need to find Peter's business partner. He has an office in town, but it is closed when I get there. I break into the office to try and find anything about him or Peter but there is nothing. It is a dummy office with a desk and empty cabinets. A light on the desk and some odd pictures on the wall but other than that no one works here it appears. Another dead end and it has me so mad and frustrated.

I decide to head back to the burlesque since it is open all day and night with several shows going. I can hide in there and wait for Timothy to show up. So, I head back to the building, stopping to get fresh clothing from a closed shop. I need fresh clothes and a bath, but at least the clothes will do for now. I just hope this is not time wasted and that he will show up to check in on the things.

I spend several days in the building and one of the employees come and notify me as I requested. I go to the office to introduce myself and kind of corner him here. He is a proper fellow with a clean haircut and shave, he wears a nice business suit and is kind of meekly. He is not at all what I expect but he doesn't really matter. He asked me just what I think I am doing and that I need to leave at once.

I explain to him that I am not going anywhere until he gives me the information, I need to find his business partner Peter. I make it clear it will go a lot easier on him if he cooperates. He then approaches me and tries to push me out of his office. I then grab him up and place him against a wall, showing him my teeth and the hell in my eyes.

He literally pees himself and ask what the hell are you and why me. Then I explain I, like Peter I am a vampire and that I am here to kill Peter and take back what he stole from me. I can tell he knows nothing, and I lower him back down and tell him to gather himself. I tell him I do not want him just Peter and all I need is an address. I also explain when I am done all of Peter's businesses will belong to me.

After a short conversation Timothy agrees to help me if I do not harm him. He picks up the phone and calls Peter, he explains there is an out-of-town businessman here that requests a meeting with him. Peter agrees to meet the next evening at the office in town. I do not tell Timothy I know the place is a false office and I know Timothy is about to double cross me. I agree to meet them, and I leave the office.

Following Timothy without him knowing was easy. I figure I cannot trust him so I follow from a good distance so Peter cannot pick me up. He goes into the office and then a few minutes later he and Peter leave as I expect. They split and go separate directions, so I follow Peter and let Timothy go. He has done just what I need him to do and bring Peter to me.

Peter heads down the street and out of town. He walks for a while, and I follow him to what appears to be an abandoned plantation. He is walking slowly down the drive and so I think it is my time to approach him. I run up on him and before I can do anything he grabs me and throws me across the yard.

I get up and rush him again telling him he is going to die after he answers all my questions about Reina and Phillip. I ask why he set me up and pulled this elaborate plan over all these years? He just smiled and said that he will tell me as the lights in my eyes go out then we rush each other. He throws me again and walks back a bit.

Chapter 36
The Truth Revealed

He then begins to laugh as he walks around pacing back and forth. Then he starts saying Robert, my dear Robert, you should know you can't sneak up on me and you should know I am way too strong even for you to defeat me. You should have kept your distance and let the past go. He continues to pace like he is waiting for me to attack.

I say back to him that he is an arrogant bastard and that I trusted him. I jump on him again and again he throws me off like I am nothing. He says that I am going to die, and he comes towards me. We start circling looking at each other and never look away. I say to him he will tell me the truth before I kill him. He starts to laugh once again as I jump and this time duck and then knock him to the ground jumping on top of him.

He says if you want the truth then you will have the truth and he pushes me off and jumps up. Then we start circling and what he says next baffles me and leaves me uncertain of everything I know. What he says make perfect sense, but I find it hard to believe. He tells me that all those years ago that it was him that followed Reina and I to the park, and that he was the one who took her.

He explains that he was searching for a bride and that she was just perfect. Beautiful inside and out a total package. He had been watching her for a while and decided it was time to take her. He was going to leave me alone but after turning her she began to fight back, and she became too strong to control. She left without a trace and he figured she would come back looking for me.

He says he was surprised when I had come back into his life, and he thought the best plan was to become friends. He thought if we became friends she would stay away, and he wouldn't have to worry about us finding each other again. He also explains that Reina was the vampire that I did not recognize, the one that had been tracking me from a distance.

He thought he would stay friends long enough for her to find us together and then he would kill me in front of her as punishment. The more he explains the more rage that builds inside me. I am still baffled, but anger is taking over. He laughs and says I played my part well, but he does not want to keep up the game any longer.

I stand there looking at him and now he says it is time for me to die I lunge forward and bury my hand in his chest. I pulled his heart out and then I rip his head from his body. It happens so fast, and I barely remember doing it. The look that is stuck on his face says it all.

My work here is done and my business with Peter is done. I leave his body in the field for the sun to discard and I head into the house he has been staying in to see what I can find. I start by cleaning up and finding new clothes to wear. Then I go through his rooms one at a time. I find nothing for a while, and I am beginning to think this is just a temporary place for him to stay while in town. Then I come to a room where I find Reina's wedding dress and a few pictures of her. He has been hiding her here from me and tried to make her a forever wife for him.

The reason I could not find her makes perfect sense now. He brought her all the way here and hid her so she couldn't find me. He thought he could kill our true love and make her stay with him. He was convinced that the vampire bond could eventually break the love she and I have had most our lives. I am also not surprised he could not control her she is a wild one .

Chapter 37
New Business Plan

I have my revenge but that just leaves an empty feeling in my soul knowing she has been there in reach. Knowing that she has been following me but has never reached out to reconnect. Now that I know who the presence is it makes more sense why I do not fear her. I know now who is causing all the problems and I need to find and stop her. I hope to convince her to come home and continue our lives together. We are still technically married and have an obligation to each other. This takes until death do you part to a whole other level. I am pretty sure she has wanted to let me know, but she may not have been able to because of Peter. She may also have no humanity left; she is after all an old vampire by now and may hate me for not being there to rescue her.

I will find out more when I return home but before I can leave, I must meet with Timothy. I also need to see Max one more time on my way out of town. It always seems that when I get things completed on my journey something else smacks me in the face. I can never seem to find the peace I seek. One day my journey to leave my past behind me will be completed. Hopefully not with me dying as the solution but who knows.

Then as I sat in the dark getting ready to spend my last day sleeping here, I have a sadness come over me about what I have done to Peter. He after all had been a very trusted friend for years. I sat there and think of all the great times we spent together. The years we spent having our time with people and situations. He was like family but to know it was all a lie just guts me. It made me question most of my life and who was really on my side. Seems as if there were no loyal people in my life, and that I am truly alone.

I know now that my path and Reina's path must cross again but that is something I will deal with later. I must first work with Timothy to take over and manage all of Peter's businesses and properties. I was sure he will not want to stay on, but I figure I can explain to him that under my lead, things will be better for him. I also will make the point that it shouldn't matter who pays him if he is paid. I also will explain to him that he would be running day to day operations with John's help to maximize profits.

Things go better with Timothy than expected and we leave out quickly to meet with John. We go over the business plan moving forward. John is a young vampire, and I am putting a lot of trust in him, and I just hope it doesn't backfire. We spent two days working out everything and setting everything into motion. Then I set out for home to get Peter's affairs under control there. The split is going to be three ways, and so were the responsibilities of the empire we have just taken over. I tell them that if they need me between my visits to just send word and I will head back. I also convinced them both this is the best arrangement because I do not want to kill them both and start over with new people.

Chapter 38
Love Strikes

We have our final meeting at the pub to have drinks and say our goodbyes. I am there talking when she walks in and sits down at the bar. I excuse myself from the guys and head over to introduce myself. It has been a long time since a woman has caught my eye like that and I couldn't pass up the chance to meet her. I walk up and introduced myself and then offer to buy her a drink. She politely declines and ask me to leave because she is meeting someone. I apologize and go back to my table and just watch from a distance.

I continue to watch, and I am very interested to see her date is a vampire and she has no idea. He is clearly setting her up to enjoy later. He is kind of jumpy and he keeps looking around the room. You can tell he can sense us but is not sure who the vampires are. I cannot ignore her she is very similar to Reina and that is why she caught my eye. Long red hair, green eyes and a fit medium build. Her clothes do not hide her figure at all, and she will make a great bride. I know vampires go looking for a meal, but she is heavenly and should be coveted.

For the first time in a long time, I find someone who makes me forget Reina, someone who I want to pursue. I watch them throughout the night and then follow them when they leave the pub. I keep a distance, so I won't get noticed or spook them. She leaves him and walks off on her own not knowing what danger she is in at this moment. I continue to follow her to make sure she is safe. He quickly catches up to her and takes her into the nearby woods covering her mouth so she can't yell.

He starts taunting her and saying how great she smells and how great she is going to taste. He then tells her she should feel honored that someone so powerful like him chose her as a meal. I stand in the shadow for a moment listening and smiling because if he is so powerful, he should know I am here. I am not sure how long he is going to talk for, and I do not want to let anything happen to her. I decide to step out of the shadows and command him to back away from her.

He steps back and smiles at me. He shakes his head and says so you are the one I felt in the pub. You seem to be very powerful and old. Then he says if I do not mind my business, he will kill both of us instead of just her. He says because I am old, I think I can take him out, typical arrogance of the older breed of vampire. As he is talking, I grab him up and catch him off guard.

I then throw him farther in the woods and then I rip his head off and leave his body there. I return to find the girl still shaken and scared. I start trying to calm her down and offer to walk her home and keep her safe. She then says she recognizes me from the pub and is confused why I was here. She is confused by everything that just took place and it left me with a decision to make. Do I tell her the truth, or do I lie and make up a story.

I decide to tell her half the truth. I thought she was in trouble and so I followed them to make sure she was safe. I know guys like him, and they are everywhere. I then introduce myself and explain that she should be more careful with guys she leaves with. I tell her that if she is up to it, I would like to take her out sometime. I also said she can find me at the bar, and we can make plans. She tells me she will think about it, and she does not need me to walk her home. I say very well, and I leave. I head home to rest, but I just lie there thinking of her and wondering if she would come looking for me. It has been a long time since someone really got me like she has.

I should not involve myself with her with so much going on in my life but to find a great companion is just natural. We vampires know love as well and death and someone like her could be irreplaceable. She is beautiful and seems to be very intelligent just a bad judge of character. It would be a shame if another vampire takes her out before I get to see her again.

Chapter 39
A New Future

As I wait at the bar my thoughts of what if goes crazy. Will she accept me as I am, will she wait while I travel? The other thought is what if I find Reina and we get back together. Just so many what ifs, and I decide to just live in the moment and not stress so much. I am about to leave because I am so nervous but then she walks into the room. Her beauty just takes away my breath. All my thoughts just disappear, and I am lost in her. I almost don't react when she sits down next to me.

She then slowly says I was going to report you to the authorities, but I figure it would not help because you will just turn into a bat and fly away or something. Then as she laughs, the room lights up from her smile and the glint in her eyes. I have not seen someone as beautiful since Reina and I am completely hers. I cannot just tell her that but at that moment I want her to be my bride. As I begin to look to the future, she speaks pulling me back into the moment saying tell me everything and we will see where things go.

I suggest a drink and then a long walk where I can tell her what is important and answer any questions she may have. We sit for a while and enjoy our drinks, and amid this I realize we did not have a formal introduction. I stop and say I apologize but last night we did not swap names. My name is Robert and what might your name be? She simply replies that it makes sense because I did not know if she would report me or not and that she was pleased to meet me. She proceeds to say my name was Lena. It is short for Marlena, and she doesn't remember when she shortened it.

We spent a good hour talking and have a few drinks before leaving to go for our walk. We are not too far from the pub when we come across a clearing with an interesting rock formation. She stops and sits down on one of the rocks and says OK spill it. I want to know everything that led to you saving me last night and freaking me out and showing me the myth is real. I start to speak, and she interrupts saying this better be good because it's not every day a girl is threatened by and rescued by a vampire.

I told her I will give her a quick overview then if she is still interested, we can spend the next few days exploring more into my story. I start with my name is Robert Quinn, and I am older than you might think. My life has been a journey of heartbreak and revenge. I lost my wife and two people that I considered to be like brothers to me. My pursuit of killing them led me here back here. My mortal wife who I thought was dead is alive and well, but she too is a vampire, and she has been causing havoc everywhere she goes. I am on a mission to find and stop her from doing any more damage.

I said to simplify things my wife and I were attacked, and she was taken. When I woke up, I was alone, and she was gone. I had spent a lot of time trying to figure out what had happened and who had taken her. I had no idea what to do or how to find her. I met Phillip and Peter on my journey and became friends with them. Then Phillip betrayed me and, on my quest, to get revenge I found out Peter was the vampire who took my wife. I then killed both and have been trying to clean up the mess the three of them have made. The three of them were working together the whole time and she was out of control. I explain that part of me wants her back but part of me realizes she is too far gone.

Lena just sat there looking at me and then smiles. She says I suppose I can believe this story since I saw a guy turn to dust yesterday right in front of me when I went back to see if it really happens like in the myths. She then says what about us. What do you see happening if I continue to see you. If you find your wife, will you kick me to the curb like old news since you both will live pretty much forever. I collected my thoughts and realize how bright she is. I then explain that once I deal with Reina that I am looking to settle somewhere and just live my life with no more problems. I then say that I would like for her to be my bride. I know we have just met but I just know I want you to be with me forever. I would like you to consider being with me forever. I explain there is no going back and that it is a forever commitment because she will have to be turned into a vampire as well.

She again just smiles and then says, Robert it is very sweet that you would like to marry me, but we just met, and I just found out vampires exist. She then asks me to walk her home and thanks me for a nice evening and thanks me again for saving her. She then says she will need time to process all this and time to get to know me. We exchange contact information then she kisses me on the cheek and walks into her house. It leaves me confused but optimistic because she did not say no, I feel like it is good to just put everything out on the table and not waste time. I left feeling good overall and couldn't wait to see her again if she decides to see me again.

She did have a valid concern about what happens if I find Reina. Will I leave her to go backwards in my life? Would she actually consider being transformed into a monster like me just so we can be together? If she is turned will she be the same sweet girl or go crazy out of control like Reina has? So many questions to get answers to and no way to know the outcome.

Chapter 40
Another Arrogant Captain

The next evening I make my way back to the docks to find safe passage back home. This is always a process because I must find and procure a ship that can be trusted or bought. Keeping my secret is hard when travelling so I always must pick crews carefully. Upon entering the docks, I see several ships with the US flag flying on them. This is a good sign, and they are larger ships which means hiding on them will be easy for me. The next but harder step is locating the crew from one of the ships. I need some luck since I can't just hang out at the docks all day.

I am about to head into town when I see what looks like a captain leaving his ship. I approach slowly and get his attention. I inquire if he is indeed the person in charge and if I could have some of his time to discuss a business proposition. He replies that he is the captain but he is very busy and doesn't have much time. He also says if I know what was good for me, I will take off. I do not expect this level of rudeness but given how dangerous the fishing and transportation business is it will cause people to be on edge.

I then say calm yourself friend, I merely need safe passage back to the states, and then I inform him my business here is done and I need to move on. I also offer to pay well for his time and his discretion. He then tells me he doesn't care about me or my money that I need to disappear. I then say to him that I will not be polite to him much longer and that the next step will be me taking his ship and crew. I then show him my fangs and walk towards him. He does not seem phased and walks towards me and tries to grab me. I instead grab him and sling him up against a wall. Then I pick him up off his feet and snarl at him. I then say to him that I do not want to kill him, but I will if he continues to be aggressive towards me.

I see a complete change in his eyes, and I feel him begin to shake. He looks as if he is going to cry. He then starts pleading with me saying he needs to protect his crew because there has been another crew trying to take them out for about a month. I tell him that I understand, and that I can help him with that problem if he would provide me with safe passage home. He says if I can help, he will discuss with the crew and give me an answer. I ask him if he knows where the crew is that is bothering them so I can take care of them. He says he can take me and show me the bar and crew so I could try and deal with them.

He shows me their ship first and then we go to the bar in town. His crew is supposed to meet him here later, so I do not have a lot of time to deal with these pirates. He then he starts pointing out the other crew, which turns out to be several crews from different ships. I ask him if he and his crew is a bunch of children since he seems to have so many people he can't handle. He looks at me and tells me to take a hike and that he will not be insulted by anyone. I tell him to relax and let me deal with these guys that I was just pulling his chain. I figure I will need a crew of my own in order to take over this dock. I will have to deal with each ship individually. I explain I will need a couple days to fix the situation. He agrees to meet back here when it is done.

I stay at the location and wait for the crews to leave so I can follow them. They stay late which does not give me a big window to work with. They walk together for a few streets before splitting up and going their separate ways. I follow the one that heads back to the docks. I figured he will be the best one to start with. I follow him from a distance making sure he is far enough away, so no one sees me take him out. It really is unfair how quickly we can dispatch them.

I follow him to a dark and hidden area where I approach him and force him to take me to his ship. Once we reach the ship, I snapped his neck and then prop his body up near the steering wheel. I then leave a note instructing his crew to leave the area or they will suffer the same as their captain. I also suggest that they pass the word to other ships that pirates will no longer be tolerated. I then leave and try to track down another one of the guys from the crew. I was not able to find them, but there is always the next evening.

I just hope the guy I killed was actually the captain and that these guys take me seriously. If they do not I will have to escalate things to get the job done and get the other crew on my side.

Chapter 41
A New Crew

The next evening I clean up the rest of the crews which set us up to have more than one ship. I figure I can increase revenue for myself and the ship's crew. It will take time to find loyal crews to man the ships but it will be well worth it. I have one day left before heading back to the states. I do wonder in the back of my mind if Reina really is the presence I have been feeling all these years. If she is and I find her what will happen? Will I have to kill her, or can I stop her without violence? Whatever happens I am excited about a new beginning back home.

The first day back in the states will be like going home for the first time in years, even though I haven't been gone that long I will be starting a new chapter in my life, and I only have one thing left to deal with to completely move on with my future. I have a lot to organize but I still have my contacts in place so it should be a good transition. It will be interesting to see if she causes me any issues.

We have not even docked yet and her presence hits me. It is like getting smacked in the face with the first burst of cold air when you open your casket. I don't know how she tracks me or if she is tracking me, I do not know how she could have. I suppose it is a coincidence that I run into her now. I think this is the sign that I must focus on her now and business later. If

I do not, she will keep me distracted and I will accomplish nothing. That in turn will keep me from moving on from my past.

I spend several hours trying to track her down but as in the past she vanishes. Then it is just still, no one is around and no vampires at all. It is very unusual in such a populated area that there is no sign of vampires. I spend the next few nights searching for her and find nothing, still no vampires except one that had just been turned less than a week ago. He has met no other vampires except the one that had turned him. This made me realize how out of control she still is and that I really need to fix this.

My thoughts immediately go to can I kill her if need be or will my love for her keep me from stopping her. I have loved her for so long. Can I handle losing her a second time? Could I live with myself if I must kill her knowing I swore to always protect her. The answer to the question will not be answered until I find her. The best part of all this is pretty much knowing she is the presence; the worst part is not knowing what her plans for me are currently. She could take me out and I would not have enough time to prepare because I never know when she will show up.

She may not want to discuss anything if she blames me for her being taken and turned into a vampire. There is nothing I can do because I was not a vampire at the time and had no idea they existed. I do not know if she knows or cares how I suffered all these years without her. She has no idea what I went through looking for her and I have no idea what she was told all these years to turn her against me.

I am lost in thought as I walk down the road,

something I seem to do a lot. I feel so safe with my senses and my power and forget I am still vulnerable to other vampires. This was made clear when I realize I was being followed but this was a different vampire. I didn't know what they were doing but I figure I should find out. I stop and call out to whomever is following me. I say I know you are there, and it would be best for you to just come out and face me.

I stand there for several minutes and call out several times. My thoughts are this vampire works for her and is just messing with me like she does. I know I am tired of this game and I really start yelling. This game is old and I am more than done playing it .

Chapter 42
Another Lost Soul

Then I hear a very meek voice come out of the shadows asking for help. She then went on to say that I am lost and confused and need someone to explain the changes happening to me. She then says she meant no harm and just felt my presence and thought I could help. She then tells me her name is Amanda and that she is so weak and tired. She can't eat but has a thirst she doesn't know how to quench. I tell her to come out of the shadows and follow me. I will help you.

I stand there for a second as she makes her way out of the shadows, and it takes me a second to realize I am mesmerized by her beauty. She is a small framed but very athletic woman with a great silhouette. She has long brown curly hair, green eyes and beautiful pouty lips. Her beauty is like nothing I have ever seen. For the first time I really understand the phrase take my breath away. Love at first sight suddenly makes sense. She is the one I did not know I was looking for and I completely forget what I was doing.

From that moment I spent all my time with her and taught her about the changes and that she will have powers beyond her wildest dreams. I let her stay with me so I can teach her and protect her while she is transitioning. I felt attracted to her but did not feel it is the time to try and show her that. She is going through a lot transitioning into her new life. I hope to eventually let her know but we have a long journey ahead of us. We spend a lot of time changing her house to make it safe for her and we spent time establishing a new routine since she is now a woman of the night.

Spending time with Amanda made me question everything about my life. Is it really my responsibility to stop Reina? She and I have not been a couple for a very long time. What if I don't give into the games and just move on, can it work? Reina has spent years at a distance and eventually someone will put an end to her upsetting the balance of things, do I need to be involved or the one that does it? The big question is if I ignore her will she just go away?

I start training Amanda on how to get food and how to use her senses to her benefit. I explain the challenges of being a vampire and I also explain how much more she can enjoy life. The clarity of being a vampire makes things so much more enjoyable, but it can also make things more painful. I explain to her that she will have a long and incredible life if she follows my training and allows herself to get over her fears. I then tell her all the information about the woman that had turned her into a vampire. I also say that she is never far away because she has been following me for years but never approaches me.

She has a lot of questions about her, but I try to assure her that no matter what I would do my best to protect her even if it meant me dying in the process. Then she kisses me and quickly pulls back and apologizes. I was a bit shocked but pleased at the same time. I then tell her no apologies are needed. I then confess that I have wanted that for a while. I explain that I was very attracted to her and would love for her to be my Vampire Bride. I say that I did not say anything because it didn't feel right with everything she is going through. She then has a shocked look on her face, and she just sits down. Then like someone kicks her she jumps up and grabs me and said yes as she kisses me again.

I then say that I really want to be with her, but I might have to deal with Reina at some point and I do not know what the outcome will be. I promise that I was hers now and that we are going to have a great life together. In the back of my mind, I still go back to Reina and can I free myself from her for good. The only thing I know for sure is this is the first time in a long time I am super excited about someone new in my life, and I need to focus on that. Even Lena does not excite me like she does or pull out that animalistic desire.

The best part about Amanda becoming my bride is the fact she is already a vampire and I do not have to turn her. The only bad part is she belongs to Reina and may turn on me at some point if she is commanded to do so. It truly is a gamble but it is one I am willing to take.

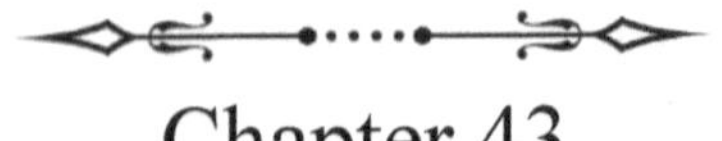

Chapter 43
The Heartbreak Never Stops

The next few months went well and there was no sign of Reina. Amanda and I are getting close, and we have started building a group of vampires. My businesses are coming together and now we are building a new coven. Amanda has adjusted very well and is independent and venturing out on her own. There are enough of us now, I know she always has someone to watch her from a distance. I also realize for the first time in a long time I am happy and feel like I am part of something great.

Years go by as Amanda, and I grow as a couple and life is great. There are no new vampires and no Reina. My life is finally levelled, and I am doing great again just like before Phillip double crossed me. Our coven has grown, and we were thriving, and life seems perfect. Of course, as soon as life seems too good to be true a thing will always pop up. That is why you should never leave loose ends just dangling in the wind.

One still summer evening I am making my way home when a familiar presence appears. A presence I have not felt in years now and honestly, I am not happy about it. I change my course away from the coven so if she is following me, she will not know where the rest of the family is located. I walk for a while, and she stays with me, so I know for sure she is following me. I am really hoping she will finally make contact.

I just run over in my head how the conversation is going to go since we no longer know each other. I have no idea how I will feel face to face with her, but I really need to tie up this loose end. We walk for a while and then suddenly, she is gone again. What exactly is she up to, is she just checking in or is she planning something big. Should I be concerned that my past is literally getting ready to blow up in my face? All my feelings of guilt, doubt and uncertainty just flood back, and I now know I can't escape the past.

I spend the next few days pondering what to do and how I can draw her out. She is always ahead of me and is always gone for long periods of time. How can I possibly get the advantage over her and am I strong enough to stop her. I know I need to bring everyone in on what is happening. I think as a coven we can deal with this once and for all. I have concerns because she made several of these vampires, will they or can they go against her.

I explain to everyone what is going on and who Reina is to me and to them. I then ask them point blank if they will fight with me or will their loyalty fall to their creator. I explain I need to know if I can trust them to have my back or do I need to handle this on my own. I make it clear that there are no ill feelings either way and that I just want them to realize I am fighting for everything we have built here together.

After the meeting Amanda and I go off on our own and I confess to her I am concerned, and I am not sure if this is a fight we can win. I am worried we might not have the numbers to fight against her because we have no way of knowing how many vampires, she has with her. I really feel it best that I handle this on my own since everyone with us is so young and may not be able to handle the task at hand. The plan is for me to go out the next evening by myself and try to track her down. If I don't return, then she will oversee the coven. I explain if I die, they will need to move to safety and stay underground awhile.

Chapter 44
The Hunt Continues

I spend the next few weeks going out and trying to find her on my own. I just walk and walk hoping to pick up some trace of her. Nothing turns up, no trace of her at all; she has just vanished again. I eventually just settle back into my normal routine, but I am always on alert now and I wonder if that is the point. She doesn't want anything more than to just disrupt my life and keep me from being happy without her. The whole coven is on edge, and it makes it hard to enjoy ourselves, but we are doing the best we can. Weeks turn to months again and the thoughts of her lessen and life seems to balance out again.

After a couple months I go to Amanda, and I tell her I feel like this is the calm before the storm and that I also feel I need to be on my own for a while away from the coven. I figure the only way to finally get her to come out and confront me is to make it look like I am back on my own. My plan is to stay at Amanda's house until after I can end the game with Reina. I need to do this for my own sanity. Amanda is not happy and tries to talk me out of it, but I have made up my mind and I leave for the other side of town. Time to start life on my own again and it really upsets me to do so. I feel like I must be punished every so often for my life to balance.

Months go by and nothing happens, just lonely

nights and hours of thinking about the different outcomes. Maybe all these years she just wanted to be us again, but she is afraid I will not find her attractive anymore because of what she has become over the years. Then one day out of the blue there she is following me. I just walk towards the local park area so I can find a bench to stop and sit on. I walk slowly just to see if she will try and stop me or just disappear again.

I sit down on a bench and then call out to her. I yell very clearly that I am tired of the games, and we need to end this. We are too old and too much time has passed. It is time for us to move on and stay out of each other's lives. I want to get closure but the only way to do that is a face-to-face with an honest conversation. I speak for several minutes hoping something will get her to come out and sit with me. I say everything I think could get her to reply but as usual she just vanishes again leaving me even more frustrated and confused.

I sit there for several minutes completely unaware that danger is close. I am completely caught by surprise when a large vampire grabs me and throws me across the park. He is big but he is a young vampire and obviously being used as a pawn by Reina. I jump up and decided to teach her a lesson about sending these young vampires to face me. I knock him back and then slam him into a tree so hard it almost falls over. The impact stuns him, and he falls to the ground. I think he figures he is a big guy and can do some damage, but he has never faced someone like me. I walk towards him and plan on ending this, but he is strong enough to get up and fight back.

We spend several minutes throwing each other

around the park. He is strong and starts talking smack, but all this did is upset me more. I gather myself and I jump up and with one clean move I rip his head off his body and then stand there for a second waiting for the body to drop. It stills bothers me that I must kill these poor misled souls, but survival of the fittest always prevails. I then move the body to a covered area.

Now I am even more upset as I walk home not accomplishing anything. I have no idea what it is going to take for her to come out of the shadows, but I need to figure it out before any more lives are lost. I need to see Amanda, so I send word to have her meet me in town. It is a short walk, but I still need to watch my back, I never know when she will show up. I hope Amanda is safe walking into town and I hope she has an escort come with her. I will never forgive myself if something happens because of me.

Chapter 45
Lonely Again

When I arrive at the meeting spot Amanda is not there but another coven member is there to meet me. They inform me Amanda had been gone several days without contact. They also tell me she had received a note to meet me, and she never returned and neither did the escort that had gone with her. I immediately head back to the coven house looking for clues as I make my way hoping to pick up something. I walk and walk but find nothing and I figure it must be Reina because the letter arrived before I sent mine.

I spend every night that week searching for Amanda and just like with Reina nothing turns up. I know nothing good comes from this. I have already lived through this and it's just as hard this time. I really worry about her safety but just like before there is nothing, I can do it's out of my control. I am the one she wants to punish and making me relive this is a perfect way to do it. I just hope she contacts me soon and that this means this is the beginning of the end.

I head back to the coven since she seems to know where it is, and it is most likely where she will send word. I walk into the coven house, and I realize how empty it is for me without her here. This emptiness is all too familiar and even though I once loved Reina I am ready to end her life especially if she has harmed

Amanda. I just hope this cycle doesn't repeat itself and I go years without knowing what has happened to Amanda.

I decide it is time to move on from the coven and search for Amanda and Reina. I gather everyone and we choose a coven leader to run things in my absence. I then leave specific instructions that I am to be contacted if Reina or Amanda return. I then leave for home feeling heavy hearted and frustrated that once again I am on a path of my own with no direction to face. Only time will tell the outcome. All I am certain of is I never want to go through this misery again. Once I get rid of Reina and this cycle of misery stops, I might just take my last walk in the sun.

Getting back to business as usual is tough and I need to expand the business in the states. Time just creep by and no matter where I am, I think of her. I will spend time looking when I can, but it becomes obvious she is gone, and I won't find her. I realize I need to get away, so I plan a trip to London to check on things there. I figure time can give me a new perspective. Who knows, maybe when I return, she will be waiting as usual for me.

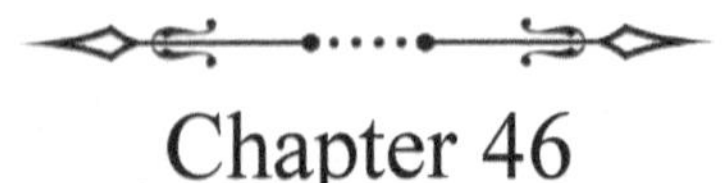

Chapter 46
Surprises Never Stop

Once I am back in London I bury myself in work, sleep and not much else. I find over time I think less about the past and can function normally. I also find myself questioning why as a vampire am I allowing myself this torment. Why can't I just be cold and heartless like I am supposed to be. I figure it is time to let go of whatever humanity I have left. Instead of being alone and sad thinking about the past I need to move forward and just be the monster I am meant to be now. Life will be less complicated if I just don't care!

Then one day as I am walking down the road I am stopped by an attractive young lady. She asks if I am Mr. Quinn, and I reply to her that I am indeed Mr. Quinn. I then ask who she is, to which she replies, it doesn't matter who I am. She then states she is just delivering a letter. Then she turns and walks away without another word. I put the letter in my coat and continue my way. There is no reason to follow her, and I can read the letter later. I am not ready to head home yet so I go to a local late-night theatre so I can watch a show.

I make it home just before dawn and do not have time to read the letter. I figure I will have time before work to open it and see who it is from. I still have vivid dreams of Amanda, Reina and the other people from my life that mattered at some point. I can't completely forget the past, but I do find it easier not to think about it while I am awake. It seems like evening shows up faster than normal and I decide to read the letter. I figure it is business related but when I open it, I am shocked to see it is from Amanda.

Well, the letter is signed by Amanda but is written by someone else and then sent to me. This means they are here watching me somehow and I have no clue I am being followed again. Strange thing is the letter is asking me to return to the states and meet up with her. I immediately figure this is a trap and Amanda was probably killed right after she signed the letter. The only way to know is to go home.

Was I really at a point where I want to return to the same miserable crap that I left there. Am I ready for whatever is waiting for me if I do return? There is so much unknown, and do I have a choice since they clearly know where I am now. I suppose my plan on leaving the past behind me is not an option. If I stay here, she will have to bring the fight here where I will have an advantage, I think. The vampire side is like you forget her and everything there except your business dealings. The human side is trying to go back in case there is a chance I can save her.

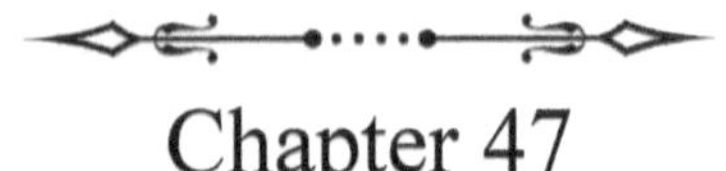

Chapter 47
Another Trap Perhaps

I spend several days pondering over what is best or at least the safest thing to do. Ultimately, I figure it is time to head home and face whatever is there so I can try and finally put all the garbage behind me. The journey back to the states proves to be a challenge like I have never seen. We hit a hurricane Mid Atlantic, and the boat is rocking side to side. I fear the ship will completely capsize and the crew will be lost. The screams and the yelling seem to go on for hours and out of the blue it is just silence. The storm passes and we have lost most of the crew due to the wind and waves beating up the ship. We are completely off course by the time everyone gets their bearings and try to get control of the ship.

I am not able to go up until it is dark and the crew that is left is upset. I didn't help during the storm, but I try to make them understand I would have if I could have. I then help with the rest of the cleaning and reorganizing what is left on the ship. Supplies are low and we need to dock sooner than later. We still have at least a day's journey to reach home and it is a quiet and somber day at sea. When we finally arrive at the dock, I am expecting Reina to be there but there is no one, no humans and no vampires. I find it odd but at least I wasn't hit with stuff as soon as I land.

It is a long peaceful walk to the house, and I am

expecting it to look like I have been gone for a long time. I am shocked to see the place is spotless like someone is living there while I was gone. This made me nervous and realize I need to find who is here. I find a place to hide and wait for them to return. I have no clue who will pop up, but I am going to be ready for them. I wait until dawn and then I go to sleep figuring that it is safe, and no one is going to show up.

I spend the week meeting with the group and checking on everything. The coven has nothing to report, and they have not seen or heard from Amanda or Reina. The truth is everything is going great, and they don't understand who would have sent me a letter bringing me home. I am getting to the point where I am going to pack it up and head back to London realizing this is a wasted trip. I begin to think someone is playing with me and it is just upsetting me beyond words.

Chapter 48
The Bait

The day before I am going to leave another letter shows up for me. Unlike the last one this one completely enrages me. This letter spells out in detail that the first letter was bait to get me home and that Amanda signed it just before her life was ended. She continues explaining that she knew I would not respond unless it had Amanda's handwriting, even if it was just a signature. The letter continues with her saying that only she is allowed to be with me because that is the way it is meant to be. Then she requests we meet face to face to work things out and she is tired of us being apart. She knows now I am strong enough to protect her unlike before and she is ready for us once again.

There is going to be another letter instructing when and where she wants to meet. I used to dream of this but now I just want to destroy her for the hell she has put me through. I spend several nights out trying to track her down because I do not want to wait for her. I want to end this now and I figure this is just a trap so that she can try again to kill me. The truth is I am as dead inside now as my body is and if she does kill me great, but if she does not, I will never again seek out someone to be close to. From this point on I am going to just be what I am a creature of the night, a monster hated and feared.

I at that point enter the darkest era of my life as a vampire or mortal. I did not wait around for the next letter. I just left town and went on a huge spree of killing for no reason other than letting out my frustrations and killing the remains of my humanity. I become all I was meant to be, and it feels good to just let go and not care about what tomorrow will bring. I travel for years taking what I want and neglect my businesses and everything I have spent years building. Time flies when you don't care and when you're finally making the most of every day.

Then one night I am out, and just as I kill someone and start to hide the body, I get the sense of someone watching me. It is an old familiar presence, but it is faint, and I cannot place who. I walk out of the tree line and there standing waiting for me is Amanda. She is looking at me like I am an animal, and she seems horrified by what I have just done. I must have been a sight standing there covered in blood and I don't remember when I had bathed last. She stood there for a second staring then she starts crying asking me why? I start to reach for her, but she runs off saying stay away until you get yourself together.

She says from a distance that once I get cleaned up, she wants to talk and find out why and what has happened to me. Then she is gone, and I am left standing there and everything that has happened over the last few years just hits me like a ton of bricks. The look in her eyes just destroys me and the reality of the situation smacks me in the face. Reina has lied and has once again controlled my life, sending it into chaos. I am suddenly aware that the one I love has just seen the monster in me. What should I do and how do I find her? So many things hit me at once and I just go home to think and get cleaned up.

All my fears and all the years I preached about how our kind should live just blew up in my face. I was a walking hypocrite and I had no good excuse to give her when I finally get to talk to her. I hope she is able to see pass what I have done and she is willing to give things a try again. I have missed her so much and she means the world to me but at the same time do I need her or anyone at this point.

Chapter 49
Regained Control

I take a scalding hot bath and then I lay in my casket until evening comes back around. It of course is not a peaceful slumber for the visions of everything I have done haunts me. Everything humans hate about vampires is who I have become and there is no way for me to fix it. I must decide now whether to change back to who I am or can I leave Amanda behind and just continue being the monster of the night. I also do not know how Amanda can possibly forgive me, and I also do not know how she found me.

The next evening, I get dressed up for the first time in years and head back out to where I think Amanda might be. I walk slowly and try collecting my thoughts. I am not sure how to explain everything to her, but I need to try. I am taken aback as I approach and see her standing with another guy looking very comfortable. I immediately get mad and start yelling as I approach, asking what the hell she is doing with someone else? She quickly turns and yells back telling me to go away and go to hell while I am at it. She continues with how dare you yell at me and act like you have the right to be jealous.

This of course upsets me even more and I almost lose it on the guy, but she gets between us and tells me once again to leave. I can tell by the sound of the heart beat the guy is human and has no idea who he is dealing with, and I have no idea what she is doing. I again more forcefully try and get her to deal with me, but she gets even more upset and walks away with her human pet and starts ignoring me. I start to follow but then she turns around and smacks the hell out of me and says I will deal with you later.

A big part of me wants to snap right here and kill them both but then the vision of her face from last night hits me. I realize I need to back down and wait for her to come around. I do not want to make it worse so I just turn and walk away still upset but hoping she will follow. I walk a while thinking and realizing I may have just lost her all over again because I lost my temper. I sit there a while thinking and I am about to leave when she walks up yelling again. She wants to know what the hell is going on and where the hell I have been. She wants to know why I abandoned her the way I did.

I tell her very bluntly that what is going on is that the woman I love is standing here alive with a human after I was told you were killed years ago. I then explain I spent the last couple years grieving and living life with no remorse and with no intentions of ever trying to love anyone again. She is shocked to find out I was told she was dead and that's why I had left. She then explains she felt the same way and she is trying to hide amongst humans so she will not have to deal with losing someone that she loves as much as me. She explains that she was taken and then told I was killed and not coming back for her.

Chapter 50
Full Circle

She then says she loves me for the man I was and now that I have let the monster out that she can no longer be with me. She wants to continue the path she is walking and that we are done. I tell her she is foolish to believe a human life will ever be possible for her and that when her pet finds out what she is everything will change. I then remind her that she had promised to be my bride forever and that eventually she will have to return. I then tell her to do what she likes but don't expect me to be there when you come back crying.

That very moment I walk away from her and everything else. I sold all business ventures and decide no more relationships was best for me. I will just travel and live life with no responsibilities except for myself. I will just stay in the U.S. and not care about anything until my days are finally done. My walk to the docks will be my first one with no cares or worries. Usually I have pain or grief or guilt to deal with but not this time. If something happens or if I someone follows me, I can care less at this point I am done living life scared of the future.

Without any thoughts I make my way through the woods past an old cemetery that I know well. It is an old family cemetery that has not been used or visited in years. I am pretty sure it is a gypsy family or a family that just died out over the years. I am completely caught off guard as I approach the front gate and I am immediately overwhelmed by the presence of many vampires including Reina and Amanda. I make my way into the cemetery and through to where the main building stands, and as I approach the building, I see torches off to the side and in the middle Amanda tied to a pole. I try to get to her, but another vampire is already there and turns around and smiles at me as he takes her head off her body. Then I hear Reina say kill him as I am running towards them.

The battle lasts a good thirty minutes and I don't know how many vampires I kill but it is a lot and I never see her come out of the shadows once. She then disappears during the fight leaving her coven to die at my hands. This is one of the hardest battles of my life due to the sheer numbers I must overcome. I hope she realizes that she has just awakened a monster like she has never seen before. She may think I will always be hers and hers alone but when I find her that will be a thought she will regret.

Chapter 51
The Awakened Monster

Her plan backfires as I am mad about the attack but not about Amanda being killed. I am mad because I just want to live without all the problems that she has been bringing into my life. I leave the cemetery and don't look back, not even at Amanda's body. I just left it all there as another failed part of my past. This just goes to show how much I have moved past my human feelings, and I am becoming the monster buried inside. Reina still blames me for her misery, but her suffering is not by my doing. Her final death however will be by my doing and I will enjoy finally ending her for good.

Being back in the states is weird and refreshing because I do not have a plan of what to do with my freedom. Reina may pop up again but with less people to help her. I am at the point where I don't even care if she does, it really is a new day. Once all my businesses here are gone, I will just stay to myself and live in peace. The houses will be left to the coven except my place which is secluded and a good distance from town. It will be easier to stay off the grid and when I do feed, I have a cemetery to hide the bodies.

I get my business done quickly and then find out our coven has bought and reopened the theatre and all the actors are vampires. The building is kept dark and closed off so the daylight does not affect business; the shows can run without interruption. This business has caught the interest of other older vampires and brought them into town. It is a nice relaxing place to kill time and meet others in a civil situation. This is not one of those places used to lure humans in for the purpose of having them for dinner. This is a legitimate, professional crew of actors and stagehands.

The end of the show brought us close to morning and so I head home. I spend the next several months secluded and reflecting on where I should go from here. I know I will need interaction with someone but to date that has always ended badly for me and Reina seems to always know where I am and will never leave me in peace. I know eventually I will need to feed and try to start over with other people, but I hesitate for fear of the unknown. I wish there was an elder I could seek counsel with but there is very few vampires here and I am the only elder.

Chapter 52
Relationships

Several more months pass as I begin to desire contact with someone, just anything to break the loneliness I have subjected myself to. Being alone with just your thoughts and nightmares can drive you crazy. I can't take the quiet anymore, so I go into town to try and meet new people. The walk into town is nice and it is a clear night so I figure it will be uneventful. It ends up nice most of the way but then I pick up the sweet scent of a human female. I follow the scent and to my surprise I find an attractive young lady walking down the road by herself.

I approach her and ask why she is out here on her own. She replies that she is lost and looking for the dockyard. She explains she is supposed to be meeting her husband and friends. My thought is I can take her out here and no one will ever find her body, and her blood will be so sweet. Then the look in her face and the shyness in her gestures tug at me and I decide to escort her to the docks.

I tell her that everyone gets lost out here especially at night. I ask her if she will allow me to escort her to the docks which she hesitates to accept my help. Then I explain this area is extremely dangerous and not safe to be out here especially if you're female. She then says fine, and we make our way to the docks and to make it faster I take her through a shortcut I know. It is a pleasant walk until we approach the last alleyway to the dock. I feel the presence of several vampires approaching quickly and I make her hide. She is very confused, but I explain that she must stay hidden until I call for her.

As soon as she is out of sight the four vampires surround me demanding I hand over the human if I want to live. They clearly have no idea what they have just stepped into, and I try to warn them they are outmatched, and they will need more people if they are going to take her from me. Then a large one rushes me and then the rest follow. I throw them off one by one then I begin destroying them. In the past I would have tried to help them or avoid killing them, but these days I don't care about that. I left their bodies just piled up in a small part of the alley knowing the evidence will disappear without a trace.

Then as I turn, I see her watching and that beautiful smile was replaced by a look of horror and confusion. She is in shock and as I start towards her, she runs down the alley screaming trying to get away from what she just saw. I quickly get in front of her, and she just stops and turns away yelling stay away from me you monster. Then I quickly grab her and tell her to stop and listen to me for a minute and I will explain. She then runs the other way again yelling how can you do that, you murderer. I must quickly get in front of her again and this time I tell her to stop. You can't leave until you hear what I have to say.

I make her sit and calm down for a minute then I explain everything in detail to her. I tell her that the four guys are vampires and if I had not killed them, they would have killed both of us. She then asks how I am able to kill them so easily and I then explain that I am an elder vampire and that I am stronger than they were. I make it clear that I want to feed on her as well but since I had lost the love of my life that I did not want to put her husband through the same pain as I went through. I find that is the worst kind of pain and that you never really move on or live after.

She then says that she doesn't care and that she will head to the docks without my help. She makes it very clear she doesn't want anything to do with the likes of me and she walks away. My first thought is to just feed off her and leave her with the rest of the bodies but instead I just head into town and if something happens to her, I have nothing to do with it. I walk for a while until I come across a vampire bar and so I go in and sit down.

Chapter 53
Good Deeds

I sit there for a bit just enjoying the crowd and the noise. It seems like it's been forever since I just sat there and enjoyed myself with no worries, and no stress. Then I feel the familiar presence of vampires I know come in for a few minutes and then leave. I am not sure what they are doing but I just hope they are not waiting for me when I leave. I just enjoy a few hours of company and then decide I should head out before it gets too late to leave. I head outside and as I expect I am approached on the street, but it is a young lady from the bar wanting an escort home because it is so late.

She is extremely drunk, so I take her home with me and put her in a spare room I have. I remove her shoes and tuck her in, so she won't get cold until she wakes up. I leave her a note by the bed and then I lock myself down in the basement so she can't find my casket and freak herself out. I am a bit worried about her being in the house, but I know nothing can happen during the day hours anyway, so I go to sleep.

To my surprise when I wake, she is still there and waiting for me. She gets up out of the chair she is sitting in and then comes up and just stares at me. Then she turns and sits back down and lets out a sigh. She seems a bit confused and so I ask if she is ok and if she needs anything. Her comment stuns me as she says yes,

I need to know if we had sex and if so, was it good you bastard. I then explain to her that we did not have sex and that you approached me extremely drunk last night. You couldn't tell where you live and so I brought you here and put you in bed. I figured you could safely rest here and leave when you awoke. There are clothes your size in the spare room if you need a bath.

Then I tell her I have to head into town if she wants to go, I can escort her home if she doesn't want to stay. She turns and walks down the hall and then comes back and says thank you for the offer, but I'd rather go home to bathe and change. I then ask if she needs food since she has been awake awhile, she says yes but she will get something in town. Then we get ready and head into town. We walk and talk and get to know each other a bit. She seems to be very nice, and a pleasure to be around when she is not intoxicated. We walk up to a local diner, and I open the door for her to walk in, and then I say it has been a pleasure and start to walk away. She stops me and asks where I was going, she says she doesn't have money and ask if I can pay and stay with her a bit.

I walk her home after she ate and then I leave her even after she invites me to come in and spend more time together. It is hard to say no but I don't want to stay and get close to her. I bid her farewell and say I am sure we will see each other again. Then I head back to the pub, and I spend the next several weeks going in there just to be around other people. I did not see her anymore and I am torn about that because I was concerned about getting close, but I really need a steady companion. Then one evening as I go to leave the house there sitting on the porch is the brunette from a few weeks ago. It startles me because I did not smell or sense her at all. Regardless I ask her why she is here and why she came out here in the dark. She then tells me very bluntly that she isn't afraid of the dark and that any guy that protected her when she is drunk deserves to know her when she is sober. She then explains she thought it would be best to meet me here so we wouldn't be interrupted. I then tell her I appreciate the compliment and then I tell her that she should be scared because there are things out here that will kill her without hesitation.

She says that it is worth the risk because she thinks I am a good guy, and she wants to know me better and tell me thanks since she had forgotten. I again thank her but assure her I am not a good guy and that I am not someone she wants to get to know. I then convince her into walking back to town and explain to her that under no circumstance should she ever come out to the edge of town without me and that we can meet at the pub. She continues to try and argue, but I insist she listen to me. I once again explain that there are dangers she don't understand, and I need her to stay safe when she is not around me. Then we go into the pub and spend hours just talking about her and what all she has experienced.

Chapter 54
Truth Revealed

I realize I need to head out and I offer to walk her home, but she says she is not ready to go and that I shouldn't either. I apologize but explain I must leave and that I will see her again soon if that is good with her. I leave and make my way home and into my casket for the day's sleep. My dreams are of her and then I slide back in time again thinking about all the others I have been involved with. I realize though I am letting go more and more which is good because it allows room for more and better experiences. I just need to keep my life simple. It is one of my biggest rules I can't break.

I don't venture out for a couple days because I figure the less I go out the better chance of me keeping my sanity and I limit the chances of Reina finding me again. Just as before, I awake to find her on my front stoop waiting for me. I inquire as to why she did not knock or come in and make herself comfortable, instead of just sitting out here alone. Her reply is she knows my room is in the basement and she didn't think I would hear her knock. She also thought it would be rude to just walk in unannounced. I try telling her again that it is not safe out here for her and that she needs to stop walking all the way out here at night. She then asks me what is so dangerous that I keep trying to make her stay away, she doesn't understand why I don't want her here.

I tell her on our way to town that I am not trying to keep her away. I just want to keep her safe from the evil in the world. I tell her there are bad people all over this area that can't be trusted and some that will harm her just because she is getting too close to me. I try to convince her without telling her everything about who I am and about my situation. She is very confused, but I don't really give her an option other than listening to me. We spend the next several evenings together and I must keep leaving her at the pub in town.

We meet at the pub, and she asks me a bunch of questions I am not ready to answer. She starts off asking why I never come out during the day, and why I never eat when we are together. Then she asks what I did for work and why do I sleep in the basement when I have such a big and comfy bed. She is tired of talking about herself and wants to know everything about me now. I am not sure the best way to answer her. I give it my best try. I tell her I just prefer the night life and since retiring I move to a liquid diet for health reasons. I prefer the basement because it is quiet and cooler than the upstairs. My lifestyle is unique, but it works for me. I ask if there is anything else she wants to know. The same as before we sit there for a while then I leave.

I stay away from town for a while, and I do not see or hear from her which surprises me. I am beginning to think my last conversation with her did the trick. I leave out one evening on a dull and dreary night. The moon is covered by clouds and there is a light mist in the air. I am making my way down the road when I feel the presence of several others close by, and so I decide to check in on them and see what they are doing. I can track them easily and they are on the edge of town heading towards the main road.

I am taking my time because I figure they are just out feeding and causing mischief. Then as I approach where they have stopped, I pick up her scent and I know now they are tracking her, and she is on her way to my house with no clue she is in danger. I hesitate for a second because my vampire side thinks, good. She brought this on herself for not doing as she was told. The other side says she is a great person, and I can't let them harm her. I then decide to rush in and save her and hopefully this will make her understand.

I move in and stand in front of the group before they can reach her. I give them a very simple warning that they need to move on and leave this human alone that she is mine. I very clearly explain to them that I will not allow them to harm her in any way. The big one of the group just chuckles and says I should go about my business before they make me regret meddling in theirs. Then one of the others tells the leader that they should leave because I am clearly an elder and too strong for them to challenge.

The leader just stands there glaring at me then he instructs the rest to move me since I did not want to move on my own. The one who tried to warn them leaves and then the other two try to jump me. I easily grab them and throw them back at the leader. Then, she comes walking around the corner and the leader tells the other two to grab her and he will deal with me. I quickly move to stop them, and he moves in to stop me. Then she realizes that she is in trouble and starts running while they are trying to get to her. I struggle to throw him off, he is stronger than I thought, and it took a little more effort than I expect. I am able to break free long enough to stop the others just as they are about to grab her.

I grab the two and I throw them back towards their leader. Then I quickly jump on him and throw him back against a tree. I then try to give them one final warning that if they do not leave, I will kill all three of them. They regroup and then come for me again saying they are done playing around. I immediately grab the first one and swing him around hitting the other one almost knocking his head off. I then grab the big guy and jumped in the air slamming him into the ground. Then I turn around and I proceeded to dismember the other two. I then give him one last chance to leave before he meets the same fate as his buddies.

He is a very proud vampire and decides he would rather die than back down and so he lunges at me one final time and I quickly move sideways and grab his head and remove it from his body. I then make my way over to where she is sitting. She is crying and terrified by what she has just experienced, and she is confused by what she just saw. You can see it in her face and tell it by the way she is sitting there in shock. I try to reach down for her, but she quickly backs away and just sits there staring at me.

Then out of the blue she just stands up and starts walking towards my house. I just follow behind and make sure she gets there safely. She completely ignores me all the way there and I suppose she is trying to process everything that just happened. Then when we reach my house, she just sits down on the steps, and I ask her if she is ok. She then yells how can I be, ok? You just killed three guys and you did it with ease. I tell her I can explain after you calm down if you want me to. She becomes upset and says I don't know if I want to know, and I don't know if I want to see you again but now, I am afraid to walk home. She then looks at me and says how could you just kill three men like that with no remorse, no hesitation?

I tell her let me get you a drink and then I will explain to you why what you saw is not actually what happened. I walk with her into the house, and she sits in a chair. She kind of slumps over and her hair falls in front of her face. I leave her there and go and get her a drink. When I return, I hand her the drink and then explain everything to her.

I tell her that the three guys were not guys but vampires and that they were going to kill you. Those kind of guys are why I keep telling you not to come out here without me to protect you. If I had not been there you would be gone and nobody would ever know what happened to you. You have to be more careful and stay in town at night unless you are with me.

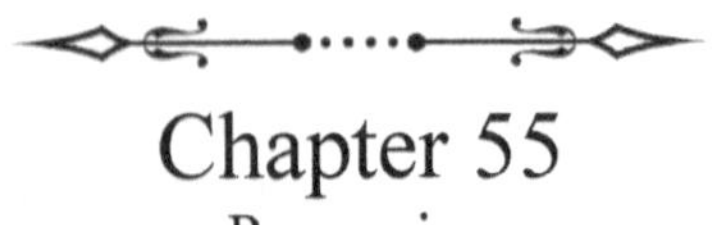

Chapter 55
Processing

Before I can say anything else she looks at me and says you are one of them! That is why you said you were not a good guy, that is why you only come out at night and have a liquid diet. Everything now makes sense, and I don't even believe in vampires existing, but now I do know they are real. She then goes on about how it's crazy all this time she has kind of been involved with a vampire and that I could have killed her at any time. She just rambles for a few minutes, and I let her because she is clearly processing the information. Then suddenly, she stops and says wait, are you going to kill me yourself? Why did you wait and draw this out between us? She says she is beginning to have strong feelings for me and now she doesn't know what to feel.

Then I explain that I never had any intention of having her for dinner and that I was beginning to have feelings for her as well. I tell her I was just looking for someone to spend time with and then you came along and here we are. I continued by telling her that I was avoiding her because of the feelings I am beginning to have and that I want to avoid hurting her in any way like the rest of the women that have been in my life. I then tell her that my love for my mortal wife makes me hang on to my humanity, the main thing that dies when you become a vampire. I spent years looking for her and lost a couple of other women I loved due to the fact I dared to love someone besides her. I found out she was also turned into a vampire and has spent the last few hundred years stalking me and killing everyone special to me. I continue telling her that I fear she is being watching and if we get too close, she will be next and that is why I didn't want her walking out here, especially alone.

She interrupts me and asks why she is doing that instead of just facing me one on one and working things out. I then explain that my belief is she blames me for her being a vampire since I couldn't protect either of us and she wants me to be lonely and miserable. I spent years running from her and my past and I have been free of her for a couple years and I want it to stay that way, but I know it will not. That is why I want you to keep your distance, and that is why I have tried not to get too close to you.

The last thing I said to her before moving across the room was, probably best if we did not see each other anymore because I couldn't stand anything happening to you. She just sits there in a trance for a long time, so I read a book and let her process. I know it is a lot to take in and I have no idea what to expect from her. Then after a while she just jumps up like someone kicked her and she runs over to me and asks can I become a vampire? Can I become like you so we can be together, and I can just stay here with you. She continues saying she doesn't care about my past, she only cares about a future together and she knows I will protect her.

I stand there in shock for a minute then I tell her no, that there is no way in hell I will bring her into my world. I tell her there is no way I would let a beautiful person like her become a monster like me. I try to make her understand she would regret it eventually and I don't want her to experience that burden. Then the conversation shifts to her being an adult and capable of making the decision about what she wants her future to be, and she figures the only way to stay safe now that she knows everything is by being here with me where Reina can't get to her. Her thoughts are logical and as much as I don't want to turn her, it is her decision now that this is thrown in her lap. I tell her she needs to take time and contemplate what she is asking and decide if she really wants to give up so much stuff in her life. I agree to do as she wishes as long as she has taken time to decide and is ready to live a life in the dark like I do.

Chapter 56
Decision Made

Several days go by and no more mention of her becoming a vampire and I am hoping that means she has made the decision to not pursue this path in her life. This life is a curse, and no one should willingly enter it knowing there is no way to go back if you decide it's not for you. I would give anything to go back and change everything that has happened and erase all the pain. She does not fully understand what she is asking, and it would be best for us both to move on and distance herself from this life. Then one evening as I sat reading, she comes up and says I am ready to make the change, I want to be like you. She says she wants to make the change now and not waste any more time because she wants to keep her hair, body, smile and youthful spirit forever and share it with me. I sit there for a minute stunned but not surprised that she has made this decision. I then tell her if that is what she wishes then I will turn her.

The next evening, we move forward with her transition into a life of darkness. I make her check one more time that she understands this can lead to lots of issues down the road and that after the painful transition she may not be the same person she is now. She said she fully understands and that she is ready to move forward. I lay her down on the couch and then slowly bit into her neck and start draining her blood.

The sweetness of her blood is indescribable, and it is almost like that first taste all over again as her blood rushes into my system. I feel her body going weak and her heartbeat starts to weaken as the seconds rush by us. It is hard to stop once you start drinking blood this satisfying, but I must be careful not to drain her all the way to where she will not be able to come back.

After the transformation she wakes up with that all too familiar thirst and need for human blood. We leave out into the night for the first time as a vampire couple and before I can teach her the right and wrong way to hunt, she picks up a scent and is gone. When I catch up to her, she is almost done draining her victim. Blood is dripping down her cheek and I have to stop her from finishing him off. She doesn't allow me to explain the rules of feeding and disposing of the bodies. She can't control herself at first and the coldness she shows surprises me. There is no humanity at all left, she has become a full vampire and held onto none of her human side. I was wrong to think such a sweet girl would need time to fully transition into a killer, but she does not even blink an eye.

That night my dreams are of her and the monster I have released into the world. My dream is the chaos and the slaughter she will bring to the world now that her real self has been brought to the surface. All I feel watching this play out in my dream is that I need to stop her before it becomes an issue. I realize that someone's inner monster is just beneath the surface, and they are looking for an excuse to let it out. I can't believe my thoughts are going so crazy and I wonder if what I have dreamed will be the reality of our situation. I guess time will tell and I will have to watch her closely.

Chapter 57
The Monster revealed

The next evening while we are out hunting for a meal for her I start to see what I saw in my dream. She is a full-blown vampire, blood thirsty with no cares about being seen or about humanity at all. She really has become someone else and is hell bent on just feeding. Anything I thought that could be between us slips away with each passing moment. This beautiful, caring, intelligent, and quick-witted woman is just a monster now. We were out for several hours which gave me time to think things through, I decide that on the way back things must change. We were almost back to the house when I stop her and say my love you must try and remember who you were before I changed you. This monster you are letting out cannot continue to be. You have to get your animal in control if we are going to continue this journey together. She then says that I am a weak fool to think we can be anything other than this powerful god like person. She then tells me if I cannot deal with her like this then she will leave, and it will not be my problem anymore. After a moment of thinking I say please forgive me my love. Then I grab her and pull her head from her body without any thoughts or hesitation. I can no longer be responsible for releasing this monster out into the world and not controlling it. It hurts deeply to do this, but it is for the best. I lay her body by the tree line just enough for the sun to dispose of it. I say my goodbyes and head into the house.

I sit there for a while and think I must be missing something. There must be information that can help decide once and for all where I fit in the world. Another one of my failed attempts at love and one crazy one still out there somewhere waiting to add more misery to my life. I need to find answers and I can only do that by getting back to my original task of finding out more about vampires and what that means. I am so conflicted about everything I have experienced and do not know what path I must take. I keep returning to the same thoughts of just ending myself once and for all, but I do not have the courage to do so.

Chapter 58
The New Quest

After several days and hours of deep thought I make the decision to start over. I will go back to Romania and begin my search for Vlad again. Romania has hidden secrets and I still need answers. On my own I will be able to move quicker and hopefully turn up something. I know it's dangerous going on my own and if I do find him and he doesn't want to be found it could end badly. It is a risk I must take and if this trip turns out to be nothing as before I will leave it all behind and disappear into the night once and for all. It is time for this endless cycle of my past to stop once and for all.

The last time I visited here we landed in Constanta and headed straight to the castles known to be tied to Vlad. This time I land in Mangalia and decide to visit castles that were old and possibly abandoned or turned into museums. I will be going at night so there shouldn't be anyone around. My route will take me north through Bucharest and then onto Lulia Hasdeu going through Ploiesti. From there I will continue to Cantacuzino Castle and then Rasnov Citadel. I will have roughly six more castles that are around the same time frame as Vlad but if he is immortal, he could be anywhere. I feel like this is going to be a long, drawn-out journey. The countryside in Romania is beautiful but treacherous on foot so I must be strategic while travelling. If I can find transportation I will have to go back to Constanta and then west to Bucharest to pick up my journey as planned. I think going straight across the country to Ostrov and then crossing over to Calarasi will be the fastest way for me and I can go undetected. I figure if there are any obscure castles along the way I will check them and sleep there as well.

It took a full night's walk to reach the river crossing at Calarasi. I wish I could see it during the day. The rolling hills and river must be beautiful during the day. I really miss being out during the day and feeling the sunlight on my skin. Romania really is beautiful, and it is sad that it has such a miserable legend attached to it. I know my time is short and I have a lot to do while I am here in Romania. I will have to be careful while here waiting to cross the river and avoid daylight. I do not sense any other vampires, just humans. I would love to give in and feed, but I must wait until I am in a more remote area and hopefully, I can find someone separated in the countryside.

It took me three days to reach the Castle Lulia Hasdeu and what a sight. It almost looks like someone giving the middle finger to someone. The tall middle building and the shorter outside buildings built in a common style from the 1800's. It is smaller than I imagined, and I do not know about the history of it. I should have researched it further so I would know how to go about getting in and out without being detected. Vlad may have died or at least went off the grid in 1476 but it's possible he could be hiding in a smaller and newer castle just to stay hidden.

The good thing is the open structure would make it easy to access and the smallness means I will spend less time searching, unless there are hidden chambers deep in the castle. I am able to spend several hours walking through the building. Whoever lives here must be on holiday because no one is around, and it looks like they have been gone for a time. The castle is beautiful inside and the decorations look rather expensive like real royalty lives here. I search everywhere including the library but there are no hidden rooms, doors or passages. This castle is a dead end and gave me no information or clues to where Vlad may be.

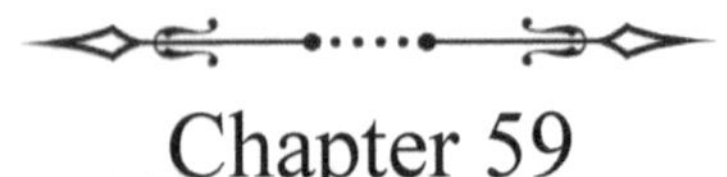

Chapter 59
The Unexpected Surprise

I leave and head to the next castle which is even newer. It is Cantacuzino Castle and I believe it was just built and would have no information but could be a good place to hide until I can move on. It takes several hours to reach, and it is a huge castle with a modern design. I want to live in something this magnificent. The high concrete wall and the watchtower wing on the back of the castle are beautiful. I'm sure it looks even better during the day, but the arch windows and outside molding are a work of art. I will not need to search this property, but I hope there is an outlying building I can sneak into and sleep.

The back of the castle backs up to the forest and I am sure I can easily make my way through the woods unnoticed. There are people here and they would not appreciate me just welcoming myself into their home. I would love to see the inside of the property I may have to return and explore when I finish my mission. I need to make my way to Peles Castle to continue my search but it's probably another night's walk and I need to feed soon. I hope that at the end of this journey I find what I am looking for. Too much time and too much pain to end up with nothing again.

I reach Peles Castle and I am amazed by the magnificent site. Even in the dark it is an amazing structure and very active. I will have a hard time examining the inside, but I need to find a way to gain access to the basement area of the castle. I realize I will need to pose as help or delivery in order to gain access so I will have to observe the castle for a couple days and figure out the best option. This also means I need somewhere to hide during the day preferably on the property.

I find a secret passageway that leads down underneath the fence on the outside wall. The walkway seems to go down under the castle as if it is used for service or events but seems as though it was sealed long ago. I make my way down slowly because I am not sure what to expect at the end of the tunnel. It is completely dark and there is nothing, no rooms and no hallways, just a straight walk to a large open room that appears to be directly under the main hall of the castle. I will need to have light so I can check for other doors or passageways in this room.

The next evening, I observe from a distance but there is not a lot of activity. No one coming or going so nothing to give me any options for going into the castle. Times like these I wish the old rumors of Vampires erasing memories was true. I would be able to enter and leave and no one would ever know I was there. I will have to be a little more patient and wait until I see some activity and just be ready to move in when the time comes. The next step is to find something to use as a light down in the tunnel. I find an old looking torch in one of the tourist booths located on the back side of the property. This will help me settle in, down in the tunnel and maybe find a way into the castle that is not detectable by anyone.

Walking down the hallway with the light is a

different journey since there are drawings all over the walls. It appears to be a story unfolding as you walk further into the tunnel. The story is in an ancient language, and I have no idea what it says. It is a lot of writing though and if I can find someone that can translate the writing, it could possibly give me information I need. When I reach the end of the walk the big room has drawings instead of words and it seems to be of a ceremony, or of a religious ritual.

I spend several hours looking at the drawings and searching for any hidden doors or passages. The only thing I find is a hidden switch that raises a ceremonial pedestal with a knife displayed on it. The blade seems ancient and is covered in dust. There did not seem to be anything else hidden in here, so I push the button and returned the pedestal to its resting area. This cave has to offer more clues or another way into the castle, but nothing is making itself known. I will need help and there is nothing else to gain here. I will need to get in the castle if I hope to find anything relevant.

Right after sunset I wait and finally find a way into the castle. I know it is a gamble but hopefully it will pay off and I won't get discovered. The place is just as beautiful inside as outside and there appears to be priceless artifacts everywhere. The person who lives here is either a serious collector or has been around a long time and collected items from every era. I am really hoping it is the latter, but I am not sensing any other vampires here now.

This place has several small tower-like additions and one large tower-like structure at the front, but I doubt I will find anything there. I will need to find not so obvious doors or hallways that are either roped off or locked from everyone. If someone is hiding here, there should be some small signs that will point me in the right direction. With a little luck this will be the final stop on this journey, and I can finally head off into the sunset with the answers I am looking for.

After several hours of searching and trying not to be seen I find a locked door that seems out of place. I look around for something that I can open the lock with. It takes a bit of time, but I find a key in a hall drawer that fits the door perfectly. I proceed slowly through the door into the darkness hoping I won't startle anyone or anything. After a few steps I find another lantern on a table and I am able to light it. When the light hits the room, it is amazing ancient furniture and a bookcase with what appears to be ancient books. After several minutes looking through them they all seem to be religious or books about witches and black magic.

I think I find the second piece of the puzzle for the cave down below. The second door leads to a hidden passage that went through the walls beside the hallway. I follow them into another hidden chamber with the same markings as the chamber below. There must be a connection or passageway between the two areas. There didn't seem to be anything, so I went back to looking through the books. Several of the books do seem to be out of place so I open them to find hidden artifacts inside of them. There is a cross, headband and bracelet with a chain that appears to connect to the cross. Whatever is happening here is very hidden and appears to be lost in time.

I continue to search the bookcase and find some hidden latches that allow the bookcase to swing out. Behind the case is a rack of hanging robes that have not been touched in years. Very elaborate and seem expensive, the finest materials. I am really thinking that I found something that has nothing to do with my journey but has my interest. Now I am thinking I will figure out a couple different things on this journey. Ancient rituals and vampire history.

I find a black book hidden in a box inside the passageway and it looks really like the book of wizards. The myth is that witches and warlocks controlled the demons from hell using this book. The witch's rituals were said to revolve around satanic worship and the understanding of how the devil really operates. This all makes sense now, the chambers and robes. All the markings and books fit into place. Everything here belongs to witches and warlocks of the past and ancient demonic rituals were performed here. I now realize that maybe Vampires were a result of one of these rituals and I need to spend time learning all the rituals they used in the days of old. The biggest problem is finding someone to translate the books and the markings for me.

Perhaps finding Dracula would still solve all the puzzles but I still have no leads for him. My research may uncover more answers as I research the past here. Finding someone who knows of the ancient world in a land that is still driven by the past shouldn't be too hard. I will need to look in the older part of the city and maybe deeper in the walls of this castle. It seems I just find more questions than answers.

I continue to search the castle but find no passages or clues. I will need to stay here until the next evening and since no one comes through here I figure I am safe to sleep here in the temple. I find a small area to crawl into and sleep so if someone does come through here, they will not find me. I am starting to get a bit frustrated with the lack of answers and I am not sure where to go next. The only logical move will be northwest through Bucegi Mountain. Mountainous and dangerous but there is history, there is places where things, or people can hide. I will need to find passage across the river and will need to feed since I will be alone on the climb. I will need to find some materials to research or maybe a guide to go with me to find any ancient ruins. You just never know what past will come back to haunt you.

Chapter 60
The Last Clue

My first destination will be the Heroes' Cross located at Cairaiman Peak. It is a new structure built to honor fallen soldiers, but I wonder if this location was built to hide something underneath. I don't believe I will find anything, but it is a great start and a sight to behold. From here my next stop will return me to Bran Castle to do a more extensive investigation. This castle must hold some secrets. It was used as a mainstay for Vlad and must be a place of comfort for him. We will see if I come up empty again.

The journey up the mountain is not as treacherous as I had imagined. The path is mainly clear, and we pass several beautiful waterfalls. They are breathtaking and mysterious. The Foamy Valley Waterfall and the screaming waterfall better known by the name Cascada Urlatoarea. We even pass through several little camps; people just set up to help outsiders go safely through the mountains. The mountains are full of beautiful peaks and valleys with the best of nature sprawled out in front of you.

It only takes us about 5 hours to reach the cross and make camp. I then let my guide leave so that he won't be stuck here on the mountain with me. I really overestimated this trip, and I am very happy it is faster than expected. I spent several hours researching the area around the base of the cross. I go into the underground area where people would not normally go and find nothing. I realize there are no answers here and I will need to continue to Bran Castle. I estimate that I can reach the Castle within a few hours and that I should be able to hide until I can get inside and start searching deeper in the castle.

Now that I am standing in front of the castle, I realize my journey has gone full circle. As a young vampire I came here searching for answers, looking for Dracula or something to give me the answers I needed. I have spent many years searching and have found nothing or no one to help make any of this make sense. I think about all the travelling, all the fighting and all the heartbreak and wonder why. I hope that this magnificent castle will open her secrets and let me finally see.

I spend what seems like forever combing through the castle. So many rooms and hallways to look through. I spend so much time looking for anything hidden or anything that stands out. This was where the myth and the rumors began. This is where the famous Vlad Dracul became Count Dracula. There is so much history here in this one place I must find something. I keep searching until I find a hidden crawl space under a carpet in a roped off section of the castle. The opening reveals a ladder that goes deep into the darkness.

After reaching the bottom I find a hidden hallway that is carved into the rock under the castle. There are several rooms and chambers along the pathway, and it appears that no one has been here in many years. As I reach the end of the tunnel there is a split into two separate areas and there is no light, so it was hard to decide which way to go. I decide to head back up top to find a lantern to use so I can investigate more thoroughly. It seems to be a lost passage with a lot of hidden clues to uncover.

After several more hours of going through the tunnel and checking out the rooms I find one that has recently been used. There is also another passage that leads out the backside with a heavy wood door. In the room is a set of caskets and several boxes. The first casket is a plain one that has not been here long from what I can tell. The second I am very familiar with because it is the one I put the metal pieces on all those years ago. I slowly open the first casket to find it empty and then I go through the boxes searching for clues to who was here. The boxes are new and undisturbed. I start finding clothes and papers that are new as well. I find maps and letters between two people with no names mentioned.

As I read through the papers it appears to be notes or plans about areas and people that this person has been studying. I continue to look through the boxes and then realize that the handwriting seems familiar, it seems as though this person may be someone I know. Then after the last box I decide to check inside the other casket and under the cloth at the foot I find a book. I open the book and I am immediately shocked by what I am looking at and wondering how this can be, I now have more questions than answers. What I have here is a complete recording of a journey that started many years ago. A journey that mirrors my own, one that now pulls everything together. I only flipped through a few pages and realize this is Reina's Story!

www.ingramcontent.com/pod-product-compliance
Lightning Source LLC
Chambersburg PA
CBHW031625170726
47990CB00017B/371